ABOUT TH

Janet McNeill was born in Dub   .... was
minister of the Adelaide Road Presbyterian Church. In 1913
the Rev. William McNeill was appointed to Trinity Church in
Birkenhead and the family moved to England.

Janet went to St Andrews University where she took a Classics
degree while writing and acting for the university's College
Players. She was awarded a First class degree and stayed on to
take a Masters' degree. Her father had returned to Northern
Ireland in 1924 but health problems led to his retirement from
the Church in 1930, as a result Janet moved to Belfast where she
was employed by the *Belfast Telegraph*. She first worked as typist
before becoming secretary to the proprietor, Sir Robert Baird.

In 1933 Janet married Robert Alexander, at the time the chief
engineer in the city surveyor's department, and left her job to
start a family. Janet had received a typewriter from her father
(who knew of her ambition to write) as a wedding gift but she
would not write seriously until her children were at school. The
Alexanders moved to Lisburn where they built a house named
Hawtree and brought up four children.

After winning a BBC competition in 1951 Janet McNeill began to
write. Initially she focussed on radio plays, which were regularly
broadcast on the Home Service, and several of her later novels
began as plays. In 1953 she suffered a brain haemorrhage and
after recovering her first books (a novel for adults, *A Child in
the House*, and *My Friend Specs McCann*, a children's book) were
published in 1955. Alongside her writing Janet McNeill also
served as a Justice of the Peace (for the juvenile court), acted as

the Chair of the Belfast Centre of Irish P.E.N. and was a member of the advisory council of the BBC from 1959 to 1964.

Better known as a writer for children, her character Specs McCann was the basis for a newspaper cartoon strip (illustrated by Rowel Friers) while she wrote the libretto for a children's opera *Finn and the Black Hag* (based on a short story by Eileen O'Faolain), Janet McNeill's adult novels portray the emotional dilemmas and conflicts of middle age. She published ten novels for adults, including *The Maiden Dinosaur* and *Tea at Four O'Clock*.

In 1964, after her husband's retirement, the couple left Northern Ireland to live in Bristol. *The Small Widow* was the only novel she wrote outside Northern Ireland. It was published in 1967, and anticipates many of the concerns of the 1970's women's movement in its awareness of the restricted role of women in the traditional family and marriage.

Janet McNeill continued to publish children's books until the mid-1970's when health problems stopped her career. In 1988 Virago published *Tea at Four O'Clock* as one of its Modern Classics.

Janet McNeill died in 1994.

The Small Widow

JANET McNEILL

turnpike books

Copyright © Janet McNeill, 1967

First published in Britain by Geoffrey Bles, 1967
This paperback edition published 2014 by Turnpike Books

turnpikebooks@gmail.com

ISBN 9780957233652

Printed and bound by CPI Group (UK) Ltd, Croydon, CR0 4YY

THE SMALL
WIDOW

CHAPTER ONE

Madge should have known better than to wear a headscarf for the funeral. It was not as if they were seeing Harold off at a country railway station or waving farewell to him on a windy quayside. Julia who was sitting in the back of the car wedged between her daughters criticised Madge's headgear and herself for being in any state to find fault with it. But at least Madge had got out of trousers and covered her head, and for these concessions Julia was compelled to be grateful. Harold would have found them amusing. Madge and he were cousins, had been wheeled through parks together in their prams, cut their teeth on the same rocking-horse. "Nature's Original Beatnik" had been one of Harold's names for Madge.

The car slowed, they were approaching the gates. Julia's throat tightened, the impossible thing is happening now. They proceeded up the finely gravelled avenue. Johnnie drove with a kind of pomp which was unnatural to him. Ah, poor Johnnie. Julie was glad that she couldn't see his face. She ached to escape from the pressure of her daughters' hips, the inevitability of shared warmth and the threat of shared emotion.

Madge untied her headscarf and pulled at the ends, then jerked them into a tighter knot below her chin.

So far the funeral had been mercifully odd, offering a succession of small items to grasp at and entertain the mind. Julia had been uneasy about the short service. How would the children react to it? Only Liz, in her fierce Do It Yourself way,

7

was religious—"I doubt, therefore I believe". The others might feel embarrassed or outraged. But if they did they showed no sign of it, and the clergyman's words, instead of desolating the heart, proved reassuring and lent decent unreality to the thing they were going to do. It seemed possible that Time's Ever Rolling Stream might collect Harold and leave the rest of them with damp eyes but dry feet.

The car drew up, was joined by other cars. They got out and were exposed to the wintry air. Ralph and Johnnie, Sam and Lionel took up their burden. Lionel handled it more expertly than the younger men. Why Lionel, who was Harold's cousin, instead of Charles, who was Julia's brother? Probably there were rules and the men knew about them. She hoped Charles wouldn't be offended, he was accustomed to the front row; he had flown over from Ireland this morning, was going back tonight. Julia had hardly spoken to him except to express regret for any inconvenience that Harold's death was causing to his routine.

The mourners formed into an untidy procession and started in the direction of the grave, trying to find a pace between a stroll and a trot. The raw wind robbed them of any attempt at dignity. It plucked their hair and their clothes, snatched the breath out of their mouths and ruffled the tufts of frozen grass. Only the humped shapes of the dead were undisturbed.

Julia dodged her daughters and set off beside Madge. The rear triangle of Madge's scarf whipped noisily.

"All right, are you?" Madge mouthed sideways, offering comfort and the distant knowledge of cigarettes and her spaniels.

8

"Yes, I'm all right," Julia lied, suddenly feeling terrible.

"Good for you. Nearly over now."

"What did you say?"

"I said—nearly over now."

Madge seized Julia's hand and pressed it, then slipped to one side to allow the girls to take their places beside their mother. The action was unexpected and upsetting, since it was not in character. Madge, for all her devotion, never touched you if she could avoid it. But Julia wished Madge had stayed beside her, it would have been easier with Madge. It was too late now, the girls had closed in to left and right of her.

The children were terrifying this afternoon, they had no mercy on her or on themselves. It was years since they had presented such a united front. Ralph and Johnnie, Liz and Sheena, four relentless and dedicated orphans, demanding a formal come-back from her, the Mother Figure, whom they had discarded years ago. It wasn't fair. Julia felt that she needed protection from them.

Harold would have protected her. You would, wouldn't you, Harold? You would have excused me from feeling the things that I know I should be feeling, the presence of death, the shocked finality of loss. I'll do my mourning for you later, Harold. Just now I am getting through this the best way I can. You could have coped magnificently with my funeral, Harold. I don't know how to cope with yours.

Her eyes filled with self pity as she saw herself as Harold would have seen her now, too small, too fragile a figure, altogether inadequate for the tragic role. Harold's Little Woman image of his wife was often irritating but it gave him a great deal of pleasure and it would have lent comfort to her today. Harold would never have allowed these things to happen to her. They were out of scale, it was all a mistake, she should not be here, she ought to have been excused, she had got a part in the wrong play. Madge, stalking along in her unaccustomed skirt, with her large clever features bound up in knotted silk, fitted the scene better than she did. Harold liked to see his wife in soft pretty clothes. Sometimes when she looked at her ageing reflection (she was fifty-six) she felt like a monkey dressed up as a little girl, and wondered whether he saw past the frills to the monkey. It hadn't been easy to decide what to wear today. Her wardrobe, when she ruffled through it, seemed only to offer her clothes for an all-the-year-round garden party. But she had found at the back a discreet hat and coat of midnight blue that seemed in a woolly way to express a certain hope of the resurrection. She wished she could remember how she had come to buy clothes like this and hoped Harold would have approved. He could hardly expect frills at his funeral.

It was disconcerting to think so clearly about Harold and not know where to direct her thoughts. Where was he? Certainly not below the polished surface of the lid that as it travelled in front of her reflected the steady movement of clouds overhead. The symbolism was too obvious, whoever was producing this drama was laying it on too heavily, Harold would have thought so. She glanced at the racing sky but it denied knowledge of Harold and made her head giddy and her stiff eyes swim.

It had always been important to Harold that she should

know where he was when they were apart. Whenever he was lecturing away from home the phone rang unfailingly in the evening, and Julia left the fire, the sofa, her kicked-off shoes, the glossy magazine that smelt as inviting as the supper collected haphazardly on a tray, and padded to answer it, adjusting herself to Harold's necessities on the way.

"Julia, my love? I'm speaking from my room in the hotel, got in half an hour ago, not a bad run up once I was on the motorway, but the fool drivers—the idiots one meets. Room Sixteen, the one I always have here, looks out over the roof of the dining-room. Cream of tomato flowing in at the moment with a hint of sole coming up at the rear. I'll wake up to bacon, sausage and egg." He was saying this to carry her through the night with him and make sure she was there when he woke. "The pain? Not to worry. I've taken some of the stuff. The gas fire's going full blast and they know how to look after me here. I'll give it ten minutes and then go and collect a drink before dinner, see if Luscious Lucy's still behind Ye Olde Oake Barre."

Then "How are things with you?" with no interval for her to tell him before he said the few phrases of love for her, the things he always said, recited as if he was reciting his prayers and the performance was more important than the meaning of the words. After that the childish ceremonial long-distance kiss and a sense of mission accomplished. And for Julia a glimpse of him standing with his hand still on the receiver, taking stock of the pain (an old war wound in the groin) and when he was sufficiently sure of himself stroking his nostril with his forefinger and pulling at his waistcoat as he set out for Luscious Lucy, which he was now entitled to do since he had made it a joint enterprise. Sexually a very shy man he enjoyed this kind of long-distance male parade. Because Julia had loved him for three years with ardour and painstakingly for thirty she allowed herself to see him with Luscious Lucy's eyes, a large man of sixty, his head thickly thatched with stiff grey hair, prancing a little pompously in an effort to make his movements lighter as he crossed the floor, his kind colourless eyes on the lookout for any reflection of himself in the eyes of strangers.

When he had left home four days ago he couldn't promise her a phone call. Julia was in the hall helping him on with his overcoat. They had just finished an early breakfast.

"I'll try to ring, dear, but I may not be able to manage it. We'll be rehearsing the thing all morning—split second timing, you know—and then there's the performance in the afternoon and the television affair and after that the dinner. It could go on quite a while. So don't worry if you don't hear from me."

"I won't, Harold."

"Promise?"

"Of course I promise," Why make a thing of it? I love you, I love you but I can't give you ardour at this time in the morning. How do you do it, or is it just an essential part of the farewell routine? I suppose the Little Woman's concern makes you into a larger man. Of course I won't worry. I'm as tough as nails really, it is you, for all your size, who are soft and a worrier. It suits me sometimes to be fragile but I reserve the right to choose the times myself. In her irritation she eased his overcoat clumsily over his lapel and the row of medals clattered and threatened to tangle.

"Mind the Christmas decorations, dear," he said, making a joke out of it to kill the possibility of any other joke. He set them in order lovingly and bent to lay his cheek on her's, asking for a general and unspecified indulgence. She gave it patiently, blaming herself for needing patience. He pressed her against him and held her, trying by his bulk to possess her, but his body felt distant and only half realised inside his overcoat, like the embrace of a snowman. She heard Johnnie's step in the porch and prayed that Harold would let her go before he came in.

Johnnie lived in the garden flat and appeared at irregular intervals and always without warning. Julia prided herself that she had grown accustomed to the arrangement, had rid herself of curiosity when days passed without a sight of him, knew how to smother her fury of love when he came. "How nice for you," her friends declared, "still having Johnnie at home. These attractive bachelors, it's madly unfair! No, I didn't understand a word of that play of his but I read what it said in the papers."

He came in wearing a sweater over his pyjamas; heavy hairy body, spindly legs, like an animal from the zoo whose hind quarters dwindle disappointingly. He knew something was going on right away; even in his pram he'd been jealous of his father. He took note of the dark suit, the city overcoat (normally Harold wore rather racy clothes for an academic) and remembered the occasion. He smiled.

"Ha! The Old War Horse snorteth and scenteth the Battle!

He paweth the earth with his hoof and heareth the Bugle afar off!"

Harold's face assumed that flat look it took when the children made fun. Then it relaxed, surrendering to his love for the boy.

"That's the general idea," he agreed, "Operation Nostalgia."

Julia snapped "Don't be an idiot, Johnnie. Just be glad you weren't born in time."

"I'll have my chances. Book me a petal in advance, Dad. But we'll watch Madge and you on the telly and our bosoms won't half swell with pride."

Harold brightened and he said "Thanks, son." Oh God, his innocence and goodness!

Liz, the elder of the girls, who inhabited a flat on the top floor came downstairs very quickly and neatly, organised to catch her bus by a split second, wearing as she always did her little skin of personal distance between herself and other people. She worked in a Welfare Office in the city. Today her straight uncluttered hair followed her movements like obedient seaweed. Julia's hair used to look like that in the privacy of the hairdressers, before the Marcel wave was laid on.

Liz reached the hall and said "Hallo, Mum. Hallo, Dad. Hallo, Johnnie," without slowing up.

"I'm just off, Liz," Harold announced, yearning for her blessing. "Madge is calling for me, we're using her car. Want a lift?"

"No, thanks all the same, Dad. I'll stick to the bus. And I'm staying at Eleanor's place tonight by the by."

14

"Got your poster ready?" Johnnie asked. " 'Remembrance Day must go! No more Glorification of Slaughter! The Future, not the Past!' Get yourself arrested if you can, then we might see all three of you on the telly."

Liz stopped. Her cheek—didn't the girl do anything with her skin except clean it?—grew faintly pink. Johnnie had always enjoyed making her rise.

"Be quiet, Johnnie!" Julia ordered against her better judgement. Already her head ached. She wished they would all take themselves off and she could go upstairs for aspirin and sit about in a blessedly empty bedroom, bouncing gently on the unmade bed with a cigarette and the newspaper, until the back door and the clatter from the kitchen told her that Mrs. Parsons had arrived.

"I'll get arrested if it's necessary," Liz assured Johnnie evenly.

"You do that," he recommended, "but put your trousers on first, it looks better on the telly. Is the Passionate Preacher going to be there?"

For reply Liz snorted. She opened the door. Unexpectedly the morning was thick and noisy with November rain.

"It's raining!"

At once they went into the argument routine as if they had been cued for a tribal dance, knowing they were being ridiculous but unable to behave otherwise.

"You can't go out in that!"

"Why ever not?"

"Tell her, someone!"

"An umbrella, haven't you got an umbrella?"

15

"It isn't as wet as all that."

"Not wet? She'll be drowned!"

Be quiet, be quiet. Why must we do this? She has eyes. Let her be drowned if she wants to.

"I can't be bothered with an umbrella." Liz pulled a plastic hood from her pocket and cocooned herself efficiently and unattractively. Her face looked as if it too were made of plastic. How guilty need one feel for having produced a plain daughter? "Don't fuss!" Liz snapped at them.

"You could wait and come along with us," Harold suggested, "Madge is due any time."

Liz didn't answer but strode off into the rain, leaving the door wide. They heard Madge's horn on the road. "Madge," Harold said, "there she is." He reached for his overnight case with one hand and Julia's shoulder with the other.

"Wouldn't do to keep Florence Nightingale waiting," Johnnie said.

Liz had come back. She stuck her head in to announce "That's Madge. She's at the gate."

"We heard!" they cried ungratefully.

"Come with us," Harold said, but Liz was running for the bus stop. Harold set off down the drive. Julia couldn't recall any significance in that final moment of Harold's last goodbye. It was unfair that he had gone away like that, extricating himself from a tangle of family irritation, unfair that she remembered only relief when the front door closed at last.

Suddenly Johnnie said "He's forgotten his umbrella!" The umbrella was lying on the hall table, rolled and ready.

"He won't need it, he's with Madge."

"He meant to take it."

She picked the umbrella up and stood undecided. "Mustn't get your little feet wet!" Johnnie said in a skilful imitation of his father. He took it from her and made off through the door. She went to look after him, calling "Johnnie!" He didn't turn.

"What about your feet?" she cried peevishly. His bedroom slippers slopped through puddles, his naked heels shone pinkly in the rain, he pranced like a clown, enjoying his performance, brandishing the umbrella and hallooing.

Frayed with impatience Julia came back into the hall. I ought to be better at this sort of thing after all these years. I used to be able to do five tracks of thought at once and get all the answers right. But I'm too old for it. In any case they are adults now, there's no need to be umpire for them any more. It's their turn to be right—let them get on with it.

She tried to detach herself from the emergency at the gate. There were voices and presently the sound of the car driving off and of Johnnie's footsteps returning.

He came through the hall without looking at her and went at once into the kitchen. She followed. He was crouching in front of the stove, steaming gently. When he shook his head the surface of the stove hissed from the scattered drops of rain.

"You caught him?"

"Yes."

"How wet you are."

"He'd have been wet without his umbrella," he chided. You never knew your way with Johnnie. Suddenly kind and considerate like that. Harold would have been pleased.

"And how was Madge?"

"Madge? Oh she was all right." There was a quality in his voice that she didn't recognise.

"What do you mean—all right?"

"Well—she always looks so different in uniform, cleaned up and starched, the crackling bosom, almost female. You know!"

That isn't what he means but that is what I am going to get. When we are so transparent to each other we must allow ourselves the use of blinds. It's the only way, anything else would be unbearable. Neither of us asked for this curious relationship, we have to make the best job of it we can. To him I'm not a person in the ordinary sense of the word. I was typecast the minute the cord was cut. I have been drained and diminished by motherhood. I am a collection of attitudes, a pocketsized matriarch whom it is traditional to have around. I have trained myself in the habit of being agreeable. I try to stick to the rules. I haven't read the books, they would be too clever for me, but I play it by ear and by heart, and am intelligent enough to get the gist of it out of the glossy magazines. One of the rules is that I mustn't use anything I remember about them as children to enable me to interpret them now. It doesn't help these self-made creatures to remember they are the children of my body. I have done my job. I am allowed, expected, to love them still, but at a decent distance.

All the same it wasn't fair. Rebelliously she asked "What did you come for, Johnnie?"

He turned and stood up, spinning, with his sodden bedroom slippers cutting arcs on the floor. He ran his fingers through his hair, collecting the last of the raindrops and scattering them. He smiled expansively. "Food! I forgot to buy any food yesterday."

Food, the elemental function of motherhood. He has come back to Mummy to be fed. He knows that Mummy will be charmed and enchanted because this is one of the ways in which she is still given a chance to love him. He thinks she's going to fall for this. She felt twisted with love for him and decided to fall, reserving a small area of her mind which recognised and criticised the game they were playing. If she was breaking the rules it was the fault of the kitchen, its intimacy and homeliness, of Johnnie's blue striped pyjamas— nursery colours—the points of light from the open stove falling on his hair and hands and feet, the stirring life in the fire, the sharing of enclosed peace.

She brought a towel. "Your hair first." He bent his head, butting against her shoulder, nuzzling. She rubbed vigorously, taking pleasure in being rough, smelling his hair and skin. "There!" She pushed him away from her. Now the frying-pan, the coffee-pot, the eggs, the tangible proofs of love. He was watching her. She remembered him at the breast and felt silly with joy.

Suddenly he said "Just a loaf. A loaf and a bottle of milk. That's all I need."

I have been too eager. I never learn. What would you do if I hit you? Sometimes it helps me to imagine impossible things like that.

"But, Johnnie!" The frying-pan in her hands was ridiculous. Maternal glory seeped out of her. "Johnnie!" It was all so unfair.

"I'm not staying to eat. My hair's dry. You said it was."

"Surely you might as well have your breakfast here."

"I can't. Max is waiting."

She set the frying-pan down.

"Max," he repeated, making a thing of it, "you remember Max, don't you?"

"Of course. I didn't know he was here, that's all."

"His car packed up. He slept at my place."

"It was Max who wrote the music for your play, wasn't it?" she asked, hating herself for being agreeable.

"That's right," Johnnie said, "that's Max. The black one. And I forgot to buy any food."

"I'll get you a loaf, then."

"And some milk."

"Anything else?"

"Just the bread and milk."

She brought them and set them down on the table, hoping he recognised stones and serpents when he saw them.

"Thanks." His voice was flat, closed. Johnnie never had any difficulty in disengagement. When he was a schoolboy he used to shut himself up in the lavatory with Gamage's Catalogue. Even then she'd envied him.

"If you're sure that's all—"

"Quite sure."

"Go on then," she scolded, giving him an exit line though there was no reason why he shouldn't find his own way out. "Go and put on dry shoes and get dressed. Your customers will be queueing."

"All one of them. 'Bye then." He kissed her cheek. She saw

it coming in time to make her face dead to him. Madly attractive, her friends said. She supposed he was. It was interesting to admit it and be temporarily immune. She was glad when the kitchen door closed and told her he had gone.

She was scraping the congealed bacon on to the bird-table—even the birds make their demands, even the birds—when the telephone rang for the first time. Sheena, her married daughter, telephoned every morning. It was Sheena. Her voice, as always, was self-important, edgy, pathetic, against a background of dogs and babies. She was now seven months pregnant with her fourth. Julia imagined her easing her short barrel-like body against the hall table, hitching the ex-baby on her other shoulder, her fierce small-featured face with its pretty hair.

"How are you all?" Julia wondered if her voice conveyed too much or too little concern for this day's report.

"Oh—we're all right."

The rebuke was plain. Are you being funny? How can we be all right? Look at our magnificent chaos, look how tired I am, see how hard I try!

"Splendid!" Julia said bleakly. "Philippa got a good night, did she?"

"Apart from being sick three times."

"Poor little girl!" My poor little girl, my little Sheena, my pet, my baby. "Is the tooth through?"

"Not a sign."

"Can't be long now."

"That's what Sam says."

"How is Sam?"

"Sam could sleep through an earthquake."

"And Martin? Did he go off to school cheerfully?"

"Oh Martin loves school."

Since yesterday then. Yesterday morning you reported that he was white and shivering and you didn't know whether to send him. But something has happened that I don't know about, the socialisation of Martin has begun, he is the boy who loves school and I must remember that. How do you decide what you will tell me, pulling at me with one hand and pushing me away with the other? Of course I don't know the modern view on the significance of the formative years, the dangers of early jealousies and repressions, the complicated sex life of infants. The theories I learned are all old hat and how clever my children have been to make such excellent jobs of themselves in spite of old Auntie Mabel Liddiard and all. God help me to acknowledge all this with humour and not be sour.

"What about you, Sheena? Is there anything I could do if I came round? Could you get a sleep?"

"Not a chance. Don't fuss. Everything's under control." Just be a dump for my anxieties, that's all.

"It won't be long now, dear."

"It'll be ages and ages," Sheena cried. "You know it will!"

"Yes. I know."

I suppose I know, but even when it happens it's a different process, isn't it? Not an act of faith and mystery and a yielding to pain and gas and clever hands and a long terrifying darkness and a separation from your husband until you are ready for him, decent and tidy and flat with a baby in the crook of

22

your arm. You hold Sam's hand all through and count and breathe, and go through stages in accordance with the exercises you have practised, and he sees the child before you do and you award yourself marks on your performance and report to your classmates how it went with you. How fortunate Harold was spared this. He had a stern dislike of nudity. In any case I was glad to get on with it on my own—even the women of native tribes seek privacy, or is that the point and am I missing the whole argument? Progress, I mean.

"Your father and Madge got off all right."

"Oh. Did they?" Sheena obviously didn't remember they were going anywhere.

"This is his big day," Julia said, anxious for the girl to share it with her father.

There was a crescendo of dogs from the other end of the line and a baby squealed.

"The milkman!" Sheena cried. "I must catch him, we need extra. Beth drank pints and pints last night when she came in from Brownies and she didn't say and I only found out this morning and Martin upset the jug at breakfast and—"

"Run! Run!" Julia cried, and was guiltily glad when the receiver was replaced.

It rang again almost immediately. Sal, her daughter-in-law, Ralph's wife.

"Mamma dear!"

"How are you, Sal?"

"Marvellous, Mamma. And you?"

When Sal said marvellous she meant it and it was true. Julia's daughter-in-law had poise and style and the graces that her daughters lacked. Even over the phone you were made aware of her gestures, her graceful persistent affection. Such a wonderful mother-in-law, I don't know what I do to deserve it, Sal said, knowing there would always be someone about to tell her. Failing all else, Harold. Julia's sympathies spun and embraced her own prickly brood.

"I'm well, thank you, Sal."

"And wonderful enough to do me a little favour?"

"Why of course if I can." Why criticise her smoothness when you criticise your own children for the lack of it? Which do you want, sincerity or kindness, make up your mind. It is difficult always to qualify for both.

"Ralph is bringing a man home for dinner and my hair is beyond words and the Infant needs to be met coming home from dancing because the hairdresser is being tiresome about giving me an appointment—"

"Of course I'll meet the child."

"Would you? Really?" One saw her widened eyes, her small delighted hands. "Are you sure? It won't make the afternoon too awkward for you?"

The afternoon is always unreasonably awkward. One demands leisure but sometimes it yawns. Often there's a committee meeting or bridge, or I must grace a public function (as Harold's wife I qualify to be invited and I do it well). Or I go to a film, being careful to choose one that doesn't wake any hunger in me, something smooth and reassuring that I can mock at the back of my mind but that makes me feel like I do after a facial. I saw "The Sound of Music" twelve times. Other women were doing the same thing, we began

24

to recognise each other and became embarrassed and went past with our heads down. There is a modern sexy film at the local just now. I would like to go out of curiosity but it would churn me up and the family would think I was mad or slightly indecent. They don't like it when I step outside the frame they have made for me. If I go I shall go furtively.

"If you're sure, angel," Sal said.

Julia made arrangements to meet her grand-daughter.

"Of course she's old enough to come back on her own but you know how Ralph fusses about traffic. He dotes. I simply don't have a look-in."

"Don't you?" One allowed oneself that small bitchy jag. "Anyhow I'll enjoy meeting the child."

"And the Infant will adore it."

Julia wondered. The Infant would prefer the excitement of buses and the chance to cheek the conductor and watching her reflection in shop windows and staring at the pictures outside the cinema and dawdling long enough to meet the drift of schoolboys pushing their way up the hill, rude and rough, shouting things.

"How is Ralph?"

"Busy, busy. You know what Ralph is."

She knew but she resented Sal's knowledge and her invitation to share it—your son, my husband, conscientious, vulnerable, self-centred, deliberate in all things.

Sal added "He sent you his love."

She was sure he did. "Give mine to him. Goodbye, Sal."

"And bless you, Mamma."

Once again the peaceful house. Once again the telephone.

"Julia?"

Lionel, Madge's brother. Since his elegant wife had left him he had come back to live with his sister.

"Hallo, Lionel."

"What's the matter, Julia?"

"I'm tired of the human race," she said, "that's all."

"In that case will it be all right if I come round and watch the proceedings with you? The telly here has packed up."

"Yes. Come by all means. Will Boy be with you? This is his weekend, isn't it?" Boy was Lionel's only child. He was twenty-six now. His name was Mark but one called him Boy. It seemed easier to accept his condition if one called him "Boy". "Mark" asked too much, demanded an individual.

"Yes, he's here. Will it be all right if I bring him? With Madge away—"

"Bring him of course."

"It goes on later than he's accustomed to."

"That won't do him any harm for once will it?"

"I don't know. They're always going on about the importance of a regular routine." "They" were the authorities at the institution where Boy lived.

"Why on earth should you tell them? I expect Boy would enjoy it."

"He would. I'll bring him, then. Thank you, Julia. I really am grateful."

He said it humbly, which irritated her since humility didn't suit Lionel. Lionel had been Harold's best man, a long-nosed debonair junior in a solicitor's office. Julia hadn't cared for him much, not at first. He struck her as affected and womanish, a curious contrast to his sister. He seemed to expect Julia to share his amusement in the trappings of the fashionable wedding, from the moment when Harold introduced him. Julia, basking in the Glory that was Harold, resented this. She hoped there was nothing to be amused about. She had just begun to wonder if sex was funny after all. She hoped it wasn't. Her Mother had offered some dark frightened last-minute remarks about the wisdom of not expecting too much. She wondered what Harold was expecting and hoped he would know. Harold knew everything; he was particularly good with train time-tables and wine-waiters. It would be all right.

It had not been remarkably all right. At first one kept one's eyes closed and pretended. Later it was better. Perhaps there was something to be said for modern lovers who read it up and trained for it like athletes and proved their efficiency by the child born nine months after the wedding day.

She said goodbye to Lionel and put the receiver down. Mrs. Parsons was already rattling about in the kitchen, waiting to receive instructions and to give the most recent instalment of her love-life. The day like any other had begun.

CHAPTER TWO

Mrs. Parsons had a bruise on the soft part of her upper arm. She rolled her sleeve up so that Julia could see it to advantage. The evidence that a man used physical violence to his wife afforded Julia a not unpleasant excitement. Probably Mrs. Parsons knew this; she always stripped uninhibitedly and without invitation.

Sheena reported that Philippa had been sick again after lunch. No, there wasn't anything Julia could do, everything was under control. She didn't mention why she had phoned. Julia didn't ask.

In the early afternoon she attended a sale of work in the church hall. This wasn't one that she was opening, but her presence was required; in any case she enjoyed these occasions, the pleasantness, the perfumes, the voices, the cultivated sound of the teacups. She ran her critical eye over the white-gloved principal lady, envying her her red carpet, the smiles, the tea at the table set a little apart, the bouquet, the two-hour licence of graciousness. At the end of next week it would be her turn to wear white gloves to a sale—a smaller pair, she had a very neat hand. The only unpleasant feature would be the young man from the newspaper with the camera. This used to be no trouble to her—instant radiance could be turned on any time. (Think "You lovely, lovely people".) But not any longer. She smiled radiantly and there the teeth were in battalions, or guardedly and instead of coming out mature and a little mysterious she was haggish and tight-lipped. It was so hard to remember one might not be looking the way one was feeling. The children would say "I see Lady Bountiful's been at it again," kindly, because they loved her. Harold wouldn't say anything; all photographs of his wife were the one he had carried against his breast in the German prison camp.

She had tea with Mildred Trent at the sale. "You're looking marvellous, Julia," Mildred said, "you always do."

Mildred wasn't looking marvellous. She rarely did. Deep-breasted, sloping shoulders, small head, flat hair and a certain defined way of putting down her feet. This afternoon she was tired and distraught, her hair in wisps, her face shiny. She had been on a shopping expedition, looking for a suit. One of her smart daughters had been with her. The shopping hadn't been successful.

"I tried on thousands and thousands," she moaned, "they were terrible. At least I was. I was a fright in all of them."

"Nonsense, Mildred."

"I was. Cora thought so. Cora has such good taste." She pulled out a handkerchief. It looked crumpled and damp; probably she had been crying privately in the Ladies' after her ordeal. "It's for Elise's wedding. I have to have something."

"Cheer up, Millie. You've just been unlucky. Anyway, it's the bride people look at."

Mildred scrubbed her eyes. "The shop assistants despised me, I know they did. And Cora was ashamed. I wish I was like Madge and could go round like a rag-bag. Where is Madge?"

Julia told her. She said: "Well, that's nice. They'll enjoy

that. There was something about the war, wasn't there? I mean nobody looked at you provided you were covered, it was shameful to look smart. Of course it was all simply terrible and we suffered a great deal. You can't say that to the children, have you noticed that, Julia? They grudge you the war, terribly. It was all our fault and nothing we did was heroic. If they knew, if they just knew—oh the lies I used to tell them about Daddy—but one doesn't want them to know, ever." Wilfred had been in submarines.

To cheer her up Julia asked about the Choral Society. Mildred brightened at once. The Messiah was coming on very nicely this year. "You'll be there, of course?"

Of course, looking across at Mildred, magnificently anonymous among the tiers of altos, secure from all criticism, enjoying herself and her own rich autumnal voice.

Julia promised to take Mildred shopping next week. "Oh, would you really, Julia?" She left the sale to pick up Sally-Anne. Outside the Ballet school she put on her brisk "Grannie-playing-at-being-Grannie" face, because she was feeling shy. Sally-Anne came out of the gate deep in conversation with a friend. She saw her grandmother and waved, then finished talking and came over.

"Mummy drives much faster than this, Grannie."

"Does she, dear?"

"Uncle Johnnie drives faster than anybody."

"Did you know Grandpa was to be on television this evening?"

"Oh!" Unimpressed.

"That will be exciting, won't it? We must all be sure to

30

watch out for him, mustn't we?" She heard herself being arch, but she had never found out how to talk to the child. It mattered a great deal to Harold to know that his family had watched the proceedings. It was her responsibility to round them up. "I expect Mummy and Daddy will be watching. I wonder if they'll let you stay up?" She sowed the seed, and prayed that the cameras as they swept the ranks would linger on Harold tonight. "It's Juke Box Jury tonight," the child said. "Is it, dear?"

She glanced, with a twinge of guilt, at the artless line from brow to lip, the softly budding mouth, stubborn chin and her little throat. My stake in eternity. I dote, I dote. But she knew she didn't. There was no identification, nothing of herself was here. It could have been anybody's sweet child.

As she drove home she found time to refer herself to Harold as she had been doing at intervals during the day, reporting for wifely duty, wondering what he was doing at this precise moment and at this, if the stuff was keeping the pain away, whether the occasion was working its magic for him, giving him back things he had lost. She always avoided relating the early Harold to the man who came home when the war was over for fear the two images might run together and become confused. Hold on to the early Harold, keep him intact. Harold the First returned momentarily, so clearly that her hands lost their firmness on the wheel. She tightened them and was surprised to see middle-aged hands, mottled across the back, and bracelet wrinkles like infancy remembered.

Light shone from the half-basement of Johnnie's flat. He hadn't pulled the curtains across. Someone, not Max, was with him. A girl, a girl she'd seen him with sometimes, an unusual choice, plain and awkward and a little shy. Not shy tonight. She was sitting on the table swinging her legs and beating something in a bowl. Johnnie had found himself another cook. He came round the table, took the bowl from the girl and set it aside, then leaned forward and kissed her, lifting her breasts with his hands and raising her, so that only his mouth and fingers touched her. Afterwards he handed the bowl back to her and she laughed and went on with her beating.

Julia felt devastated. They should have drawn the curtains. Do they leave them apart from bravado or don't they feel any need for privacy? Anyhow, how do I expect him to behave? What would they say if I went and banged on the window and told them I'd been watching and that I was torn apart with envy? They'd feel a faint disgust, pity too perhaps. I wonder what emotions they judge proper for me to entertain. Desire is only justified by being desirable. The girl has a pretty laugh. There is an innocence about her. I am sick to death of the soft pedal.

She took a drink upstairs with her, turned on the radio in the bedroom and decided to dress up a little for Lionel; not really for Lionel but because she needed it. A softly draped dress, web-thin stockings and her small plump feet tucked into very high heeled shoes to make her legs look longer. The dress was more becoming than she remembered. She'd had a rough day pulled about by duties and expediencies. Now the house was peaceful, no sound from Liz's empty flat overhead and Johnnie fully occupied below. No more adjustments. She was glad Lionel was coming and felt relaxed, not amorous but vaguely romantic in the way that Lionel would appreciate. Lionel understood women. "When I come home after meeting Lionel I can't bear to look in the mirror, it's such a disappointment," Mildred had said. Since Isobel left him he was accustomed to spend his evenings on the other side of the fire from Madge.

She put on eye shadow and twisted the lamp shade to give herself a better view and smiled at herself and felt pleased. She also smiled at the large silver-framed photograph on the dressing-table of Harold. Lionel's coming, she told him. Of course Harold would be pleased. Lionel was the person she needed, the tragedies of his private life had given him sensitivity and an intriguing neuter safety.

She remembered the evening when he had come to tell Harold about Isobel. Harold was out, he told Julia. Afterwards he wept. In her arms his body seemed light and small in comparison with Harold's. As his weeping eased a cold embarrassment crept over them, it became impossible to separate and look at each other's faces, and so they remained stiffly interlocked long after the impulse that had brought them together had faded. She ached with a vulgar itch to giggle, and was appalled at herself. When at last he had taken leave she rushed upstairs and hooted shamefully till it hurt.

Now she came downstairs slowly in a cloud of self-created pleasure and perfume, enjoying the pompous proportions of the house. An accompaniment of lush music from the finale of a film would have been appropriate. In the drawing-room she arranged the chairs and lights as carefully as she would have arranged them for a lover and waited for Lionel.

"Lovely to see you, Lionel."

"Thank you for letting us come."

He looked crumpled and tired. Of course Madge didn't look after him properly. Mildred had called one evening, collecting for one of her charities, and there he was ironing his own shirts. Julia's hopes for the evening flickered but she poured drinks and they sat on opposite sides of the fire. Boy said "Nice, nice" to her necklace and then played on his hands and knees with miniature cars round the back of the sofa, making traffic noises. He was wearing a yellow jersey, the same colour as his hair and Isobel's.

She nursed her glass, looking down at her pretty arms, wondering if her perfume was reaching him and if he guessed her mood and whether it was going to be any good. She needed it badly now. Be good to me, Lionel, show me a glimmer. Can't we warm each other with a little romantic appreciation, it can be delicious when friendship trespasses outside its territory. That's all I want. But I want it. It's been a difficult day, I deserve something. Harold isn't coming home tonight. I must have something to bless myself with.

"Ten minutes to go before the programme," she said, "we needn't turn it on until it's time. There's a play—like all the modern plays, I suppose—too queer for words so that you begin to feel you aren't really human, or else bed. I get so tired of bed."

"Nothing wrong with bed," Lionel said, sipping his drink and staring into the fire. Sometimes he could be like this, a little coarse, not picking up his cues properly. He rearranged the cushions in his chair, discarding some of them. He

34

explained that his disc was giving him trouble again.

"Poor Lionel," she said.

It wasn't going very well. She mocked him secretly for her own consolation. The graceful amusing boy. Look at him now. There were pouches below his eyes, his hair receded in peaks from his forehead, one suspected a paunch. Harold had made a better job of middle-age than this little man. She thought of Harold basking in nostalgic splendour at the Albert Hall and wished she had a chance to bask. Now Lionel was watching her; she gave him a clever mature glance, one that she knew came off every time.

"You're looking tired, Julia," Lionel said. "What have you been doing with yourself?"

"Nothing," she cried irritably, conscious that her face had flushed. "What do you expect me to do with myself? What do women of my age do, just as a matter of interest? Or wouldn't you know?" She hadn't intended the sourness in her voice but was pleased when his slack face tightened with alarm. He'd have been safer with a romantic evening, poor Lionel.

"The family," he hazarded unhappily, "the Dear Octopus routine. Surely that keeps you busy."

"Don't be silly, they are all young ladies and gentlemen. My job is over."

He brightened and said "You've got the sense to see that. Lots of women don't."

"I see it but it doesn't push the clock round. What do I do with my time, Lionel, apart from bridge and the hairdresser and the library and getting threepence off at the supermarket?"

"Grandchildren—the re-entry of little feet and all that. The old fairy tales brought up to date—"

"Dear little Alec, Sat in his Dalek, Shooting his deadly spray?" she rhymed and giggled feeling pleased with herself. "I'm no good at grandchildren, Lionel. I try. I do try. Maybe I'm abnormal, I don't know. But I was a good mother, wasn't I? Well, wasn't I? I knew all the answers. And they had whooping cough and measles and chickenpox and nightmares (dogs and lavatory chains, never Hitler and air raids, that always surprised me) and Mother Fixations because they couldn't have Father Fixations with Harold in that prison, and crooked teeth and tonsils and I wore myself out over them—"

"I'm sure you were a wonderful mother," he said. His disc wasn't comfortable yet. He got up to knead at the cushions again.

"Try telling them that. You can't. They don't want to listen. In any case it's an offence against taste or something. You can only be to them what you are at the moment. And when they become parents they're the first in the world, nobody's ever done it before them."

"Well then—there are other things."

"For instance?"

"Some women take a job."

"The clever ones, the ones who've had a training. I'm not clever like Madge. I'm the small fluffy type." She fluttered her eyelids to disconcert him. "An anachronism, I suppose. I think that was why Harold was attracted. How would he like his 'little goose' with a brain?"

"My dear Julia you are no goose."

"You become what the people you love expect you to be. It's a duty or a habit. I don't know which. But that was the sort of wife Harold wanted, wasn't it?"

She was rather surprised when Lionel skipped this one and said "You could try good works."

She said "I think I do my share," and smoothed her skirt, thinking how excellent her legs were.

Lionel rubbed his nose and looked upset. "Have you thought of embarking on a session of sexual square-dancing? Middle-aged orgies are very fashionable, they tell me."

It was romance I had in mind, Lionel. Holding hands on the sofa, not rolling about on the floor. "I don't think orgies are quite my line," she said crossly.

"What about religion?"

"I am religious, Lionel," she snapped. "You know that."

"Oops, sorry!" He got up to refill their glasses. She wondered if he'd had many before he came.

"My religion is a great comfort to me," she declared, feeling desolate and beyond the reach of any kind of comfort.

"Cheers!" he said.

"Cheers!"

Boy came round the sofa pushing the car across the hearthrug in front of him. They lifted their feet to allow him to go past.

"Animals then," Lionel suggested. "Like Madge. Or my old aunt who smells. You can meet her every afternoon at the stationers on the corner choosing Christmas cards for her poodle to send to all his poodle pals in the square. Have you thought of trying animals?"

"Harold comes out in a rash. He's allergic."

"You are a wonderful wife," he said.

This pleased her. How kind he was! "Not a wonderful wife, Lionel. Not even a person. I'm one of those Identikit pictures that they've made up between them. They never look real, do they? Vacant—slightly mad I always think. But that's me."

"Why do it?"

How sweet that he should want to know. "For love, I suppose. I'm a favourite doll, rubbed smooth and faceless with being loved." This was a beautiful thought, a little sad perhaps but everything had now become beautiful and sad. And Lionel was sharing the mood with her, offering sympathy. Sympathy would be more relaxing than romance; all right, she would settle for sympathy.

"You always wanted to be loved," he said, "and you were. Everyone loves Julia, lucky Julia. Julia and Isobel. Everyone loves Isobel, don't they?"

She said "Of course, Lionel," politely, but wished he hadn't brought Isobel into it. She finished her glass. He filled it and his own. Boy came round again. One of the wheels had come off the toy car, he brought it to his father who fitted it on again. His mouth was wet. Lionel took out a handkerchief and wiped it dry.

"Boy had a birthday the other day, didn't you, Boy? Tell Auntie Julia about your birthday."

Boy flapped his hands and nodded his head many times very quickly, as if it were on a spring.

38

"A nice birthday, was it, Boy?"

"Nice birthday," looking at her with Isobel's eyes.

Lionel said: "Do you know what his mother sent him? You'll laugh."

Do we have to talk about Isobel? "What did she send?"

"An electric razor. And her love, of course."

There was no need for him to parade his private tragedies through other people's drawing-rooms. Indignantly she said: "But, Lionel—she knows, doesn't she?"

"Of course she knows. But tell her—just try telling her. He is twenty-six so she sent him an electric razor. I changed it for a teddy-bear and five dinkies. He likes those very much."

"Did you let her know what you'd done?"

"I didn't have a chance. I don't know where she is now—who she's with I suppose I ought to say. The postmark was London. There was a photograph of her in one of the glossies in the summer—perhaps you saw it?"

"I don't think I did. I suppose she looked extremely beautiful?"

"Isobel is extremely beautiful."

It was the way he said it. Suddenly she'd had enough. She stood up and placed her glass on the mantelpiece. "Lucky Isobel," she said, "how nice for her!" She caught hold of the mantelpiece to steady herself. She heard Lionel exclaim "Julia!" and saw that he had half risen. She put her hand on his shoulder and pushed him down again and watched him bouncing comically. She was enjoying herself. "You be quiet," she dictated, "and listen to me." She was feeling tremendous, it would be a good evening after all. "Let me tell you something, Lionel."

Boy had left his game and was watching her with his head on one side like a curious bird. "Hallo dear," she said amiably, "having a nice time are you? That's right. Enjoy yourself."

"Hush, Julia, hush," Lionel said.

"I don't see why. Give me one good reason. I am so bored with being a mother that I could scream." His alarm excited her. "The trouble is what do I do with my maternal instincts now that I'm expendable? Just sit and appreciate my children? Sometimes I don't even like them. But I can't stop re-acting to them. How do I do that? Well, come on—tell me!"

"Julia—"

"It isn't the same as weaning, you know, one dosen't just dry up."

"Please—"

Oh you poor withered scared little man. "I used to be beautiful, like Isobel, do you remember? Pretty is better, perhaps."

He said "You were lovely, Julia." She knew he meant it.

"And look at me now. Well, go on—look!"

He stared at his shoes and said "Sit down, Julia, everything's going to be all right."

"Why should I sit down?"

"You've had a little too much to drink, that's all."

"Not too much, just enough," she said, lifting her toes and balancing for a moment on her stilettos to show it was easy. She allowed a tide of Celtic sadness to wash over her. "What do you know about me anyway? What do any of you know over here? You never knew me when I was a child in Ireland or my home or my father or my mother. Those things died, all my childhood, when Harold brought me to England and you all took one look and said 'Who's this pint-sized bride that Harold's brought?' As far as you were concerned I originated when Harold loved me."

"And Madge. Madge loved you. You know she loved you right from the beginning."

"You're always like that about Madge, so loyal, such a champion. And then I had children and I loved them and I was the most important person in their lives and took all their decisions for them and gave them security and now they are grown up and if I need to go on being concerned about them I must get into a corner and do it secretly. Nobody must know that I'm worrying when my sons drive fast cars or go pot-holing or if they might be homos, or whether my daughters take to drugs or religion or are just plain dull. I leave them to it, don't I? Well, don't I?"

"It isn't like that."

"What is it like, then?"

Lionel didn't answer. Boy came and leaned against him, holding up a miniature car, spinning its wheels against his open palm; he offered it to Lionel who imitated the action and they laughed. Boy's eyes were completely empty of everything except love. Lionel spread his hand on Boy's head, gathering a tuft of hair with a rough caress. Then he let him go and Boy returned to his game.

"I envy you," Julia said. "Don't you see? You're lucky. I

can't even touch them now without celebrating a kind of sacrament."

Lionel didn't speak. Silence stretched and snapped. She discovered to her relief that she was crying. Lionel's shoulder wasn't as solid as Harold's but it served.

"I don't mean to be sour and bitchy, Lionel. But I am so tired of agreeing and fitting in."

"Not sour. Not bitchy."

"I love Harold, you know that."

"Of course you love Harold."

"And you love Isobel. Why did she go away? Was it because of Boy?"

"No."

His cheek against hers shaped the answers. It was interesting that the cheek wasn't the usual one and that the answers were not predictable. "Tell me," she invited. But he said nothing. He was breathing deeply and slowly. No ardour, she thought, no excitement, just kindness, peace, "Julia, Julia," he said.

Boy's cars swooped and turned corners and speeded, and sometimes there was a collision. Red centres in the fire burned themselves out and fell in a soft smother of ash.

Thinking over the evening afterwards she couldn't decide which of them had first remembered the television. She went back to her chair when he got up to turn the programme on. It was reaching its finale. The camera had left the rows of faces and was concentrating on the mass effect. Julia sat erect, dragging her eyes over the screen, persuading herself that one of the pale specks in the background was Harold. Lionel scoured the starched bosoms for the significant one. "Which is Madge? Can you see?" It was no use. The poppy petals were falling.

"We've missed them," Lionel said.

The music and singing mounted, brass heaped on drums and voices. Boy had left his game and was watching. He paraded backward and forward keeping time, lifting his knees and brandishing imaginary weapons and flags.

"He's getting excited, they say he shouldn't," Lionel said, and switched off. Boy stood in front of the dead screen whining, and then turned and butted Lionel in a fit of temper.

"Come along. Long past your bedtime," Lionel said. He didn't look at Julia. He brought Boy's coat and helped him to put it on, threading his fingers patiently into his gloves, ignoring Boy's deliberate awkwardness. Julia held Lionel's coat for him. "Oh Lionel, how could we?" He turned with the coat halfway up his arms and said "Cheer up, Julia. We didn't commit adultery," and she said "I noticed that," perkily, because this seemed the only possible key for a reply and was grateful to him for the cue.

She opened the door and Lionel and Boy went down the steps hand in hand. Once she felt she couldn't bear it, and called "Lionel!" but he didn't answer. When they reached the path she saw him put an arm round Boy's shoulders and pull him close and they laughed and set off.

She sat on the bottom step of the stairs, tired and lonely, indignant at being so upset. She tried to make a telepathetic report to Harold but the line was bad, she didn't think she was getting through. What do I say in any case? I hope the show went well, Harold, and that you and Madge enjoyed your share in it. I am so sorry, Harold, that I didn't see it or you, because I was bouncing on Lionel's knee at the time and we forgot and only came in at the end—you know how one does these things. Yes, it was very pleasant, thank you, it is a long time since I sat on a man's knee. Oh yes, Harold plenty of them, I am such a suitable build, you used to say so yourself. Oh no, Harold, just Lionel, just this evening.

None of this was any comfort. She wondered if it would help if she cried, but experience had taught her that there are times when tears are a physical inconvenience, especially when you are crying by yourself. She was glad when the telephone rang and provided her with a reason for action.

"Mamma? Are you going to be altogether darling and forgive me?"

"Forgive you, Sal? Forgive you for what?"

"Now, Mamma," Sal chided sweetly, "nobody can be quite as nice as all that; it just isn't true!"

"I don't know what you mean!"

"Trespassing on your precious Saturday and then never so much as a breath of thanks!"

"My dear, it was a pleasure. You know that."

"What sweet things you say. I really am contrite, but Alphonse was in one of his creative moods and then there was this dinner party. In fact they've only just this minute gone. Some people don't seem to know when to, do they?"

The dinner-party. Of course they hadn't watched. No

chance of finding out from Sal whether there had been a moment when Harold had been identifiable.

"He made a good job of your hair, did he?"

"Actually it is rather nice. And he is quite a sweetie. 'You know, Mrs. Ralph,' he said 'there aren't many of my clients I feel I can really do myself justice with.' I know he says it to everyone, but I fall, I fall!"

"Of course he doesn't say it to everyone and I'm sure you look marvellous!" None of this means anything but it helps life along. "And the party was a success?"

"Your son says it was so I take his word for it. You know what these affairs are like." Do you mean what some of my son's friends are like?

"Give Ralph my love," she said automatically.

"And his to you, Mamma."

Some day we must arrange a knock-for-knock agreement about affection. It would save us such a lot of time. But tonight, feeling meek and a little muzzy and grateful for kindness from any source she said "Goodnight, Sal," and rang off, wishing for simple single-mindedness, for stupidity perhaps, instead of this multiple image bred out of the habit of seeing other people's points of view.

When she was putting out the milk bottles she noticed that the curtains in Johnnie's flat had been drawn tightly across. A light burned within. She heard the girl laugh.

She decided to ring Mildred. Mildred would have watched the programme, would tell all there was to tell without being nudged, would comment on how Harold had looked and Madge. But it was Wilfred who answered the phone. He was sorry, Mother had gone up to bed early, she was having one of her heads. "Poor Millie." "Yes indeed," he said a little bleakly; "if it's important I'm sure she'd come to the phone."

"No, not important. I'm sorry about her headache. Give her my love."

The telephone rang as soon as she had put the receiver down. Sheena again. "Sheena dear how lovely!" she said unguardedly.

"Mum. You remember that daffodil costume I had when I was in the Lower Third?"

"I don't think—"

"You must, you must." She implied that it had been last week. "Yellow frills and a little brown paper hat on my head."

"Of course!" And she remembered the words, and Sheena twisting one leg round the other, learning them by heart, hissing through the gap in her front teeth.

She quoted: " 'Daffodils in early spring—Thoughts of Golden Summer bring!' "

" 'Summer's blooms and Summer's gladness—Bid farewell to Wintry Sadness'," Sheena capped. "That's right, how marvellous of you to remember. Gosh, wasn't it frightful? And I created it because I wanted to wear white frilly pants and we had to wear green!"

"You looked so sweet," Julia said. "Whatever made you think of it?"

"It's Beth."

"Beth?"

"She needs a fancy dress for a party. She ought to be just the right size for it, don't you think?"

46

"But Sheena—"

"It would save such a lot of work, and I could pick it up tomorrow."

"But Sheena, it isn't here any more."

"Up in the attic—in the big trunk—"

"I did tell you, dear. I was clearing out the attic."

"Oh—were you?"

"I'm very sorry. If there's anything I can do to help I wish you'd let me—" You could have done something. A daffodil costume to which you gave houseroom for twenty years. But you've thrown it out, you have had your chance and have failed by a few yards of yellow sateen.

"If I'd known you were throwing things out—"

"I did tell you."

"Did you?"

No use going on about it. Things become smaller and smaller, reduced to absurdity by their claims to importance. All the same I know I told her.

"Look—let me do some sewing for you—"

"No. Of course not. I can always rustle something up, I suppose. Don't fuss. It's just that I thought—"

"I know. I'm sorry."

"I'd told her about it. She would have looked rather sweet."

"How is Philippa?" Julia asked firmly, refusing to go on being sorry.

"I've been up and down stairs with her most of the evening. Just at the moment I think she's settled."

So you didn't see the programme either. "You sound tired,

dear." Pity fought with impatience and won. You aren't crying, are you? You always cried silently and suddenly, shocking me with the intensity of your grief. My tired brave child with the unknown child curled in your womb, and in that child the seed of other children. This business of reproduction going on and on, being fruitful and multiplying. "All right, are you, Sheena?"

"A bit dizzy and light-headed. I don't suppose it's anything."

She is allowing herself the luxury of making me just that bit uneasy about her. I wish I didn't know these things. I wish I were kind and obtuse like Harold is. I would be more help to her if I were.

"Go to bed, right away," she scolded.

"We will, we will. Heaven help anything that wakes us up tonight."

I haven't got used to that yet. I am thinking of her small and solitary, waiting to be tucked up, staring at the greyness of the nursery ceiling.

"You'll let me know how things are in the morning?"

"I will. I will."

As she put the receiver down footsteps sounded in the porch and a key turned. Liz came in.

"Hallo, Mum."

"Liz! But I thought you said you weren't coming back until tomorrow."

"Did you?" Liz was already halfway across the hall, steering for the stairs and privacy.

"That was what you said this morning, dear."

48

"I thought I'd come home."

"I'm going into the kitchen to make a hot drink. Are you coming?"

"No, thanks all the same, Mum."

Julia's head ached, the light in the hall seemed to fluctuate, swooping like a bird above her eyelids. For better or worse she asked "How did the Protest March go?"

"It didn't."

"Why? What happened?"

"People didn't turn up. Not enough people."

"Surely even a few of you—"

"The men—not enough men."

"Why?"

Liz turned on the stairs and looked at her with a curiously detached stare. "Presumably they didn't care."

She said goodnight and went up. Julia switched the kettle on and perched on a stool, wondering how many marks she had earned herself in that little encounter and irritated because, unlike those quizzes in the newspaper, there was no way of finding out.

A. The girl is unhappy and would like to have been told that I care.

B. The girl is unhappy and would like me to keep my big mouth shut.

C. The girl is unhappy and I am a fly on the wall.

A, B, or C was right. Once you looked at the answers it was obvious. It did terrible things to them and to your morale to get it wrong.

The kitchen was quiet and soothing. The kettle purred

consolation. Before she went home Mrs. Parsons had left everything clean and orderly. Inanimate objects had their excellence. You could measure your success in life by unblemished floors and polished surfaces. Some women did. Janice, for instance, achieved successes in her scullery she could never have hoped for with her husband.

A spiral of music rose from Johnnie's flat. Liz had reached the top landing and was banging all the doors at once, or so it sounded, stamping over the floor, pulling out drawers and slamming them shut. She would go on for hours. Some daughters didn't come home, their mothers worried about what they were doing in the back seats of cars. One must be grateful.

Julia went to her room, undressed, slipped on her dressing-gown and creamed her face, avoiding an encounter with her reflection. Then she knelt to say her prayers, making a report on the day that was not unlike the report she had tried earlier to put through to Harold. Now she had no trouble in getting through. The trouble was that her Father in Heaven would understand what she was explaining, no matter how she phrased it. With Harold she might have been able to get away with something more comfortable than the truth. And while she was thinking about Harold the telephone rang, down in the hall.

CHAPTER THREE

"I see the Russians have done it again," Madge said, waving a page of the newspaper that lay disarrayed beside the breakfast tray on Julia's bed. Julia had been reading the Obituaries before Madge came. She did this every morning now, secretly, with an avid interest—"After a long illness bravely born"—"Peacefully"—"At his son-in-law's residence." The children would think it morbid but it was information she was after, something that might provide a clue as to how she was expected to feel. The Memorial notices fascinated her, a whole human relationship measured and expressed at so much a word. The words were chosen carefully. "Beloved" had dignity, "darling" expressed passion, what did "dear" mean? It sounded rather stark. In less than a year's time she might choose words to celebrate Harold. Perhaps by that time she would know which words.

A corner of the paper fell into the marmalade and Madge fished it out and sucked it, then folded the paper badly and inaccurately and laid it at the foot of the bed—of Julia's half of the bed. The other half was glossy and undisturbed, the pillow plump and without a crease. Julia had been careful not to stray across the dividing line during the nights since Harold's funeral. The doctor's pills made her fall asleep at once. Sometimes waking in the dark to a sense of unidentified misgiving she had almost fumbled for his warmth and then realised the stillness of the room—no breath in it but her own—and turned into her pillow, allowing the pills to take charge.

During the day the uninhabited area of the bed made her embarrassed. One didn't think of bereavement as posing problems like this. One expected anguish, not embarrassment. (I shall feel anguish in a week or two, Harold, just now there isn't anything much that I feel.) It was puzzling to know what to do about the space here and all through the house that Harold used to occupy. Presumably time would spill over and close the gaps, like the bark of a tree when it has been cut. Presumably there came a moment when you finally realised that Harold was dead, was not any more, would not be, and that this wasn't some kind of an unpleasant game that you were playing. The doctor had been very firm about the pills. There was no need for her to feel anguish until she was ready for it.

She was glad that mourning seemed easy provided one stuck to the rules. She hadn't expected it to be so conventional. No wildness, no abandon. Harold had a great respect for convention. Everyone was very kind. It would be even more kind of them if they would let her talk about Harold but perhaps this was one of the rules. Madge who came to visit daily (being late November her work as Lady Gardener up and down the suburbs was still fairly strenuous, but she came) discussed current affairs in a brusque monologue. The children came too and gave detailed accounts of what they had been doing. It was a long time since she had been so well-informed about the children's lives. She lay in bed or on the sofa downstairs and listened and nodded. They looked at her, she noticed, with a mixture of curiosity and anxiety that was interesting in its novelty, almost as if she were an unknown quantity instead of the Rock of Ages quartered for them. On the rare occasions when they mentioned their father their voices were careful and deliberate.

She saw a selected number of visitors. They were chatty and brisk or else scared and dull, all transparent as glass; she experienced their emotions but none of her own. Some of the Senior University wives threatened to be over-knowledgeable about widowhood. They didn't talk about Harold, but the absence of Harold. She was glad when they rose to go.

Mrs. Parsons however talked about Harold. Every morning first thing up the stairs, binding on her apron, rolling her sleeves to the elbow, talking about Harold, or her version of him. Rubbish, Julia reflected, Harold wasn't like that, but was grateful to her for her ease.

She also talked about her own husband. Mr. Parsons had had a terrible shock when he heard the news. Taken like that. Snatched in his prime. ("Your prime, Harold!") It had sobered him up, he wasn't the same at all. Mrs. Parsons hinted that her nights were duller and more peaceable now than they used to be. Her beatification of Harold was tinged with reproach. "Things aren't like they used to be," she said, implying that her mistress wasn't the only one who had suffered a loss.

Madge was stamping about the bedroom like a caged beast and still on about the Russian Moon Probe. It was amusing to lie there and know why she was doing it—allow your mind

53

to dwell on the immensity and majesty of space and this pin-prick bereavement will fall into its proper proportions. Obediently Julia contemplated space in which now there was no longer any room for Harold. "You don't want this rot—you aren't listening, are you?" Madge said, switching the radio off without waiting for a reply. Her fingernails, Julia noticed, were full of someone's herbaceous border. It was a pity she had switched off. "When the Moonlight falls to Ashes" had been pleasantly elegiac. Sentimental but what is the harm in that? I must feel something. Why must you organise my grief like this? Do we all have to work so hard at it?

The children had been working hard. Something, they suggested, should be done about Harold's things. They suggested things that could be done, offering alternatives. Yes, yes, Julia said to them all; of course that would be the best thing to do, and spent a week doing nothing. So last Sunday she had come downstairs and the family had arrived in force.

Sam went with the youngsters into the garden—like a large rubbed-looking bear, Sam was, in his duffle coat, lumbering among his cubs, being funny but taking care not to be riotous. A kind man, her son-in-law; Julia liked him, except the gap between his front teeth which gave him a voracious look, especially when he watched Sheena with a sort of appetite; always a bit hard up and a bit downtrodden, but cheerful and kind, playing the fool out there in the sodden garden while Liz and Sheena were upstairs doing what they had decided was the best thing to do, and Julia was held captive in her drawing-room by Ralph and Sal, with Sally-Anne picking out tunes on the piano, hesitating maddeningly and then coming down on the wrong note. No fooling with kids in the mud for Sally-Anne.

Ralph was being more than ordinarily heavy today. It dawned on Julia that he had seen himself as the head of the family. He always dramatised himself—sternly she denied herself a glimpse of the child in the kindergarten.

She sat there disliking him and feeling uncomfortable, making automatic responses to Sal, trying to anticipate the next mistake on the piano, noticing that Sally-Anne in her Sunday clothes contrived to look sexy without a curve anywhere, hearing the children's clear bird cries and trying to catch any sound from Liz and Sheena.

"Don't do that, dear," Ralph said to Sally-Anne, "Grannie mightn't like it." He was always careful to give reasons. Sally-Anne went on playing, hissing the tune through her teeth, and Ralph looked across at Sal who shrugged gracefully, leaving it to him. So they're afraid of the child, Julia realised with private excitement.

Presently the girls came downstairs. Julia rose to go to them, but Ralph's voice reached the climax of his argument and she sat down again. Sally-Anne broke into Chopsticks very loudly, getting quicker and quicker towards the end.

From the corner of her eye Julia watched Liz and Sheena carrying large neatly tied brown paper parcels down the steps and putting them into Sam's car. And in the evening when she opened her wardrobe the space where Harold's suits had been gaped at her and her own clothes shivered. All about the house now these awkward little pockets of vacuum, so that staying in bed or lying on the sofa was safest.

"—at Jodrell Bank," Madge said. She had spilt cigarette ash on the counterpane, on Julia's half of it. She blew at it vaguely, then flipped it with her fingers leaving a grey mark. Julia made a note to take it out after Madge had gone. She was impatient with Madge, with what was happening at Jodrell Bank, even with convention. Tell me, Madge, tell me again what happened at the Albert Hall, three weeks ago. You told me in that naked box of a room at the hospital but surely it bears telling again. It concerns the death of my husband, the reason why he isn't here any more, the man whose bed and body I shared— you can see for yourself his side of the bed is empty now. This man/woman relationship is something you don't know about. You and Lionel are still in the nursery together and always will be, captive perpetual siblings, but the other thing is different. So tell me again. All I remember about the hospital is the sound of early morning trains shunting on the railway line, the staccato applause of buffers and the night sky growing paler in the upper half of the window where the glass was clear. Except for one thing. You said: "So that was why you didn't see us on television" and I felt relieved and realised there was no need to. But tell me the rest of it again.

"Did Harold say anything?" she asked, cutting across Madge's commentary.

There was a pause. Madge's features seemed to grow more solid. "No, I told you." She was seated astride Julia's dressing-stool, tilting it back on two legs.

"Don't do that, you'll break it," Julia said, "and I am not asking something indecent. I only wanted to be sure."

Madge staring at her own reflection in the mirror without

making any adjustment to it. That is something I could never do, Julia thought. Seeing myself always makes me react, that is where Ralph gets it from, it is terrible and unjust to criticise in your children the weaknesses you have lumbered them with. Madge stares, not expecting to see anything which calls for a response.

Madge comes like this, day after day, because she loves me. It has never been a secret. She fastened on me like a limpet when Harold brought me to England. When I saw her I knew at once why he'd said no, his cousin Madge wouldn't be a good bet as a bridesmaid—not old Madge, he'd said, and she's been around ever since, predictable and blunt and faithful, wearing trousers because a skirt makes her more vulnerable, doing nothing to her face so that nothing would ever be expected of her body. She used to blush when I was breast-feeding the babies, though with that productive bitch of hers it can't have been so much of a novelty.

"Madge I wish you wouldn't behave like an idiot. I am not going to weep or become hysterical. I simply want to be told."

Madge stopped pushing the jars of cosmetics on the dressing-table around as if they were a child's toys and told her. It was the same as she had said at the hospital, she remembered it now, the sentences after all were familiar. "We got to town around ten." Sometimes Julia interrupted to ask a new question. "Where did you have your meal?"

"At an A B C."

"An A B C! Harold! Why didn't he take you to his Club?"

"There wasn't much time; we had to get back."

She saw them balancing trays, perched on mushroom stools,

swallowing sausage rolls and slopped coffee. Harold was either being cross or else putting on an act of boyish ease, eating in a place like this. She wondered if she could ask Madge which it had been. Probably since Madge was with him he was putting on the act.

Madge had gone on with her story. Harold suddenly sagging, collapsing, lying prostrate in the long corridor at the back of the Albert Hall, staring up at the lights. Now Madge had come and was kneeling beside him, her glazed bosom hiding the lights.

"He didn't see me, he didn't know I was there."

"How can you be sure?"

Madge didn't reply. Julia imagined the distant music rising, the swell of the trumpets gathering to their climax. Did he know what was happening? Was he afraid? Ah, poor Harold, I think perhaps you were, but you never told me. It was in the small things that we knew each other, we were intimate through the shared details of daily habit, it would have been unbearable and indecent to have discussed our dying, one can only discuss death with strangers.

"He couldn't see or hear anything," Madge insisted. The laboured breathing, the whispered concern of a knot of people a few yards down the corridor, the music mounting unconcerned. The breathing ends and the vows we made to each other thirty-two years ago in the church at home—I remember the creases my gloves had left on my fingers as the ring slid into its place—are dissolved. Was it possible that the music did reach him, so that in the final instant glory took over from glory? Couldn't we allow him his tremendous moment? Even if this isn't true we could console ourselves with the idea that it might have been. But Madge doesn't go to church, she wouldn't know anything about the consolations of religion.

Rain beat on the window. "It's stuffy in here," Madge said. "Shall I open it?"

"No. It'll be cold. Leave it."

"Cold?"

The window whose pane was starred with drops of rain on a sky of evening blue became an issue. Then Madge said "You don't wear enough," and left it the way it was. She unzipped her anorak sliding her fingers round the neck of the thick jersey she wore below.

"I don't know what's wrong with you," Julia fretted, moving her little body about in the bed. "You never used to be like this. You don't tell me anything. I wish it had been Mildred. Mildred would have known what I want to be told." She imagined how Mildred would have given an account of Harold's last moments. It wasn't accuracy she wanted—perhaps it was appreciation. This was Harold's final breath. For years, waking and sleeping, she had paced her breathing with his. A man is lying in a corridor in a public place changing into clay. There should be something memorable to say about it.

"I am not being emotional or unreasonable or anything, Madge, and if you are afraid I won't be able to bear it then you can see, I am bearing it. The way you go on you'd think dying was indecent." Madge who had been standing at the end of the bed glowering like a shabby tramp turned away. I've shocked her. Good. Now perhaps we may get somewhere. "We will all be dying one after another, you and me and

59

Lionel and even the eternal Isobel. She's still beautiful he says, would you believe it? Death is the only significant thing left. Why do you have to be so different to me now that Harold's dead? As if you were defending yourself against me. It isn't doing me any good. And you've always been so sweet to me, Madge, right from the first, when I was a bride and crazy with homesickness and scared to death when I knew Ralph had started, and all those tea parties and visiting cards and the ghastly little maids we had who stayed out half the night. I don't know what I'd have done without you."

She held out her hand. Any other time Madge would have turned with her face alight, love pouring from her, slightly absurd and completely magnificent. But she didn't turn, not at once, and when finally she did her face was like a stranger's and she said "When someone has suffered a great loss—" in so unnatural a voice that Julia tittered, feeling lonely and sick in her stomach.

"What would Harold say if he knew you were carrying on like this, Madge?"

"I don't know what you mean."

"Oh, come off it. Anyway, do you think he'd have liked the Darby and Joan business—you know how fussy he was about his personal mechanics, Harold getting deaf or shuffling with his feet and forgetting things? And I don't suppose I'd have been very good at it. Well, would I? You ought to know—your old father nearly drove you round the bend, looking after him in his dotage, and I suppose one old gentleman's body is much the same to look after as another's whether it's your husband or your father."

"Julia!"

"I'm sorry. I have to talk to someone. I'll tell you something, I have all the wrong reactions. Do you remember the way Johnnie drove coming back from the funeral? Oh you must remember—like a madman—crazy. And I sat there digging in my nails and thought 'Oh God, don't let me be killed.' I was shaking all over when we got back, don't you remember? But it was relief. Just relief to have reached home safely and not be dead the way Harold was."

Madge ignored this and said "You don't realise it for a while. It's natural enough."

"I do realise it, that's what I'm telling you. You talk like the letters I've been having, such peculiar letters—the adjectives. Did you ever think of expressing Harold in adjectives?"

"You will miss him very much," Madge said.

"You're like a gramophone record," Julia complained, "and I wish you wouldn't talk as if it had been the romance to end all romances; it wasn't, you know. It was what Harold wanted. Of course I miss him. Not so much in bed, not yet. I've been too tired, but I expect I'll miss him more later on. Oh Madge don't look so coy and shocked. After all, he was my husband."

Madge said "I've been telling you that."

"Then I'll tell you something: just for the record bed was never a very strenuous affair, not with us, not after the first year or so. Funny, don't you think, that Ralph should be the one who was the child of passion?"

"Julia!"

"Oh for any sake—either you want to help me by talking

or you don't. And if you don't then I do and I will. After all Harold needed comfort and constancy. Anything more would have embarrassed him horribly."

Madge turned to the window, fidgeting with the catch. "You loved each other," she said implacably. "You were like torches."

"Not torches. A warm and reliable fire."

"And you have the children." Now she was a machine from which platitudes issued like railway tickets. But it was not a platitude Julia would have expected, not from Madge. Any other time Madge would have been quick to skip the children and press her own claims, but now "The children," Madge repeated, "Harold's children. You still have them."

Julia lay and wiggled her toes. "The question is," she said, "do I want them?"

She heard Madge throw the window wide and the rush of the curtains as they flew back into the room like flags. The cold stream of air washed round her and then the door opened and closed again, and Madge had gone.

CHAPTER FOUR

"From the sin-removing Lamb of God we learn the faith-inspiring truth of soul-gladdening redemption," one of the young men urged gently, in his attractive voice with the faint trans-Atlantic flavour. He ran the nail of his right thumb quickly and expertly under the fingernails of his left hand, one after another.

The second young man, whose beard looked like embroidery in bronze silk thread on pink velvet added "First Peter, one and twenty-five."

"Yes. Oh yes indeed." Julia said. She had become tired of standing, had backed into the hall and was sitting uncomfortably on the straight chair.

"Maintaining a corruption-resisting fight is the only sure and Satan-defying way of preserving a salvation-deserving destiny," the first young man announced, and changed over from his left hand to his right.

"Matthew ten and twenty-two," said the child with the beard.

They had been at this for some time and Julia was drying up on the responses. "I see," she said unhappily. She also saw that her visitors had crossed the threshold and were now in the hall. They had put down their shining cases of leather and laid their gloves on the table and they had their eyes on the door of the drawing-room which lay ajar.

She regretted that she had opened the door to them. It had

been a gesture, she was tired of being a visitor in her own house. If Mrs. Parsons hadn't asked permission to leave early she would have been there to open the door and close it again, smartly. But Mrs. Parsons was anxious to call at the doctor's surgery on her way home. She was off colour, wasn't sleeping. "It's when you get peace to sleep you can't," she said. Julia imagined her lying wide eyed and hungry beside Mr. Parsons who was still tamed by the news of Harold's death.

Moving around the house was the first mistake. She had spent most of last week in bed feeling more secure there, even with half of it empty. The empty half was her ally when the children came and stood at the foot and asked her how she was and she told them she was quite well, thank you. How interesting to be the person for whom other people were concerned. She had a feeling that the children's concern was wearing thin, she suspected discussions going on off-stage, views exchanged over the telephone. She allowed this to amuse but not disturb her. "Aren't you ever coming downstairs?" Sheena asked frowning at her brood who were bouncing joyfully on Harold's territory—Sheena was so big with the new baby she couldn't have reached them and they knew it. "My poor poor Mamma, still here. Ralph will be disappointed when I tell him," Sal purred behind her flowers. Liz looked in sometimes and dumped magazines or food and ran. Her expertise with public distress was no good to her. And Johnnie had come after lunch and sat on the bottom of the bed and played with her toes through the bedclothes—"This Little Piggy went to Market", and then he said: "It's my early closing day—let's go and see an 'X' film and gasp and stretch our eyes."

"Would you like that, Johnnie?"

He said "Not really." He was looking tired. Oh God, he's mourning his father and I am behaving badly. But I have been brave and stalwart and sufficient for so many family distresses for so long and this time—

He went over to the window and stood playing a game with the cord of the blind. "Has Madge been around?"

"Not today." Not today, not yesterday, not any day this week.

"I saw her the other day. She was looking ghastly."

"Madge never bothers with herself, you know that."

"Yes but—"

"I think they've had Boy at home for a few days. She always finds him trying."

"I don't blame her, that loony kid."

"He's really quite sweet, but Madge isn't very clever over personal relationships, is she?"

He ignored this and asked "Why don't you ring her up? It's not like her. Usually she's in and out with you all the time."

"I know," she said impatiently, "but she's probably gone hiking with her Girls' Club or something."

Johnnie chuckled. "Good old Madge."

The idea of discussing Madge with Johnnie was interesting. She said: "And yet I don't believe she knows what the word Lesbian means."

Johnnie batted the cord high and left it to rattle back against the glass. "When are you proposing to come downstairs again, O Mother O'Mine?" he asked, elaborately artificial. "You can't go on like this for ever."

65

She recognised the rebuke and accepted it. It was no use, you couldn't win. You talked to them in the modern idiom and they resented it. They criticised your small outdated mind and were then embarrassed if you showed signs of giving it an airing.

"Do you like me to be a nitwit, Johnnie?"

She could see the question ruffled him but he said, "You do it so well," and kissed her temple quickly and took himself off.

The procession of days had assumed a repetitive monotony. She discovered herself continually doing the same thing, lifting her morning glass of fruit juice, winding her watch, opening the paper, a perpetual "This is where I came in." The sky through the bedroom window brightened behind bare branches and seemed to dull into evening almost at once. Before half-past three the yellow light of the winter afternoon had emptied the picture-frames of everything except its own sad colour. The lights in the windows of the houses opposite were no sooner turned off than they were burning again. The flood of days carried Harold a little further into the distance. He came back in vivid gleams, in moments of luminous joy, she learned to be prepared for them. I am managing very well, she told herself. Everyone was still very kind. Lionel sent flowers and books. Sometimes Mildred rang up but it was to claim sympathy rather than offer it. She reported that the preparations for Elise's wedding were nearing their climax. At last she had bought a garment. "Ghastly, dear, in elephant grey, smooth like a tent. I look like an elephant, I feel like an elephant." "Then why buy it, for goodness sake?"

66

"Cora says it is the best I can do. Anyhow it covers me." Julia asked how Wilfred was taking it. Mildred sounded depressed. "Well, it's nice for Daddy that he enjoys weddings so much but all this nuptial fuss is really too stimulating for him, and the bridesmaids are the peachiest. Oh dear I wish it were all over. Cora has a way of seeing things so clearly. How are you, dear? Have you made any plans yet?"

This was a question that seemed to crop up all the time. apparently widowhood demanded plans. "No, no plans." "Much wiser to take your time and not do anything in a hurry." What does one do, in or out of a hurry? And when Mildred rang off she flipped through the pages of a magazine and turned up the transistor and took a pill in case Harold should be coming—the doctor continued to be very firm about the pills.

But this afternoon when she heard Mrs. Parsons' footsteps diminishing and the click of the gate behind her, the emptiness of the house asserted itself and became hostile and she almost panicked and wondered if it would help if she telephoned Madge and decided against it. Instead she dressed and decided to go to the drawing-room and lie on the sofa, exchanging one fortified island for another. If she didn't move around she wouldn't notice that she was by herself.

She had reached the sofa when the bell startled her and she turned back into the hall imagining that there might be some kind of answer waiting on the other side of the door. This was an omen. It was a challenge. She congratulated herself on having taken such a definite decision.

The young men were on the doorstep. She felt refreshed by

their goodwill and by the lack of that sympathy of which she had lately grown suspicious. Here they were now in the hall, still talking. They seemed very kind young men; she noticed that they had good manners, short hair and dark smooth clothes.

They were saying: "Of course your husband is a Believer?"
"I have no idea," she told them, "we never really discussed it very much," thinking of the things that Harold had believed in and how passionately and privately.

"Ah!" They seemed pleased. They opened their cases and pulled out a variety of volumes. "The Believer must be a Preacher in this world," they told her, "Romans ten, nine and ten." They enquired whether her husband was at home. She told them he wasn't.

It was her duty, they said, to recall her marriage-mate to the path of true faith. That was rather a quaint name for it, wasn't it? Harold would find it amusing—

"There isn't anything I can do," she said suddenly. "It's too late." The books they had laid in her lap spilled across the floor as she rose.

They agreed that it might not be easy, but that to the hardship-enduring preacher was granted the heart-warming reward of mercy-filled Salvation. Perseverance, they said—

Last week her own clergyman had called. And though he hadn't spoken of anything more substantial than her new rose bushes, his organ fund, his wife's asthma, she knew that he had all the eternal verities in his pocket and it was only his sensibility that prevented him from mentioning them.

"I'm sorry," she said, sitting down suddenly, this time on

the bottom step of the stairs. "It wouldn't be any good." Their faces, the furniture, the hall were all spinning gently to the tune of the words they recited. "First Corinthians, twelve," said the child with the beard and was joined by the clock striking four.

"He's dead," she said, and enjoyed their faces which were even better since they were distorted and she wasn't seeing them clearly. "Dead, dead. We had a funeral. I don't know where he is now—maybe you would. Abraham's bosom, perhaps. We used to have a little rhyme about that, quite amusing. But he's not here. You can look for yourselves if you like. His clothes have gone and his pipe and his shoes. There's a stick of his in the back hall that they forgot to take, and his silver brushes are upstairs—I hid them. But he's not here, so it isn't any good going on about it, either you or me, is it?"

They stared but didn't reply. They began to gather the books up quickly.

"Of course I was wrong about Abraham's bosom, wasn't I?" Julia said. "He didn't have the qualifications—not a hope. He's been cast into the Outer Darkness of utter desolation, he's in hell with all the other unbelievers. Well, go on, say so. That's what you're on about, isn't it?"

The key turned in the hall door and Liz came in, balancing a white cardboard box carefully on the palm of her hand. The young clergyman whom Johnnie called the Passionate Preacher (Julia recognised him from a television programme) came in with her.

Liz halted, looked at her mother with uncertainty and set the box down carefully. "Mum! What's going on?"

"These men," Julia said, "they called to see me about your father's soul."

The Passionate Preacher eyed the men and helped himself briskly to one of their books. He flipped through it, snorted, slapped it shut and returned it. Then he threw the hall door open.

"Out!" He looked magnificent, all he needed was a flaming sword. "Hop it," he said, "and quick!"

The men gulped. "We were offering help to our bereaved sister—" (this time they gave no Biblical reference)—"we had no intention—"

"I have," the Passionate Preacher said.

The men's faces were frog-like and so amusing that Julia began to laugh. And when the men had bobbed and smiled nervously and gathered their books and trickled through the door she went on laughing and was unable to stop, even though Liz and the Passionate Preacher were watching. In the end Liz had to take her elbow and hurry her to her room and undress her with furious prudery and pack her into her bed and pull the curtains and bring some more of the pills.

"Your friend—?" Julia asked, blissfully released from laughter and already on the edge of sleep.

"He's gone."

"Oh Liz."

"That's all right. He couldn't stay."

Julia remembered the cardboard box. Cream cakes. "Was he coming for tea?"

"Yes."

"Oh Liz!"

She imagined him folded in one of the low chairs in Liz's bed-sitter, his knees as high as his ears, biting into a chocolate éclair.

"Is this the first time he's come here?"

"Yes."

"I'm sorry, Liz."

Liz was at the wardrobe, rattling dress hangers noisily along the rail, hanging up Julia's clothes. "It doesn't matter," she shrugged.

How kind the girl could be. "He looked superb, turning them out. Like the angel in the Garden of Eden. Only of course he ought to have held a flaming sword and been naked."

"Mother!"

I should not have said that, it was in very bad taste and she is gravely offended. One can only talk like that to one's own generation, will I never learn? Mothers do not say that sort of thing. If I grow to be ninety and she is in her middle sixties do I still talk to her in the maternal idiom? She is adult and has cast off the relationship at her end, it seems unfair that she won't allow me to cast off at mine.

But I should have known better. Liz has all her father's physical reserve. When she was a schoolgirl and I rubbed her chest for a cough she was careful not to pull the bedclothes down far enough to expose the peaks of her new breasts, and I knew she was doing this and was just as careful to hide the joyful excitement I felt. I hoped perhaps that we might share the excitement, but how could we since it was important to her already to think that her body wasn't made or ever known by me? And now I have been stupid, her tea party is spoiled, the cream cakes are wasted and next time she sees the Passionate Preacher she will remember and hate me fiercely.

"I'm sorry, Liz. I really am sorry."

"Will I bring you a cup of tea?"

"No, dear. Liz—"

"It would only take a minute."

"Honestly I don't want one. I—"

"It's all *right*, Mother," she cried, refusing to accept comfort or offer any more of it.

Julia's eyes brimmed weakly. "I'm not really myself yet."

"No, of course not."

"It was those men, they upset me."

"They had no business to come," Liz scolded, "if only Dad—"

Julia's heart opened. Say something. Liz, my dear child. Help me.

"What were you going to say? Go on."

Liz hesitated. Her lower lip trembled.

"About your father," Julia prompted.

"Nothing. I forget. It wasn't important."

"He's dead," Julia said, "that's all there is to say."

Liz stared and said in a bold voice "So long as you know," and turned away suddenly and wept.

Even the girl's distress couldn't spoil the beautiful moment when the pills took over and the caricature of reality was blunted and Julia was aware of her body curled and warm in the bed, of the kindness of the doctor and the compassion of God.

For a moment after the door had closed the thought of the Passionate Preacher persisted. She almost turned to grope her way into Harold's territory. How odd, no man in my life now, not any more, that is all finished. And so fell asleep.

CHAPTER FIVE

She recognised Ralph's step on the landing, heard his careful knock, and felt impatient and disinclined to make the adjustments that she needed to make since she had not expected a visit from him. He had already made his adjustments and had the advantage over her. She thought of him as a child coming running, tumbling, embracing her knees, pouring himself back into her heart. He knocked again. She remembered the bliss of having influenza and being reprieved from Christmas and told him to come in.

"Hallo, my dear. How nice."

"How are you today, Mother?"

"Over the worst of it. No—don't kiss me, I might have a germ left." Ralph would have no intention of kissing her. Johnnie kissed to atone for not feeling all that she might expect him to feel; Ralph couldn't kiss, it was too much an act of committal now, probably he was more honest than Johnnie. He went gratefully to the chair beside the fire.

The young men with the books who had called with their consignment of mercy didn't know that it had included the bonus of influenza. But they must have brought the infection with them, there was nowhere else she could have picked it up.

She made a slow recovery, not exerting herself. Although it was now December no one had mentioned Christmas to her, she imagined this was deliberate. The family always came to her, she should have begun her preparations weeks ago, and had done nothing and no one had prompted her. But even in the limited world which she allowed herself it was plain that Christmas was on the way, the glossies had announced it months ago, a few carols were creeping into radio programmes. The post was full of charitable appeals, mostly addressed to Harold. She did not know he gave so liberally, most of them were for horses, dogs, cats—Madge must have put them on to him. Mrs. Parsons had reported this morning that the milk bottle tops had robins and holly on them. The long public pilgrimage to the manger had begun.

She feared Christmas and avoided thinking about it. She switched the radio off at the first syllable of a Noel. She read books from the library instead of her diet of glossies. Modern novels didn't really attract her. Going to bed at the beginning of a relationship instead of at the end seemed inappropriate. And over and over again. One wouldn't want to oneself and yet one was left with the suspicion that one might have missed something. If one was allowed to laugh—but one wasn't. But at least the books from the library, unlike the magazines, could be trusted not to be seasonable—theirs was an all-the-year-round preoccupation.

We can't do Christmas, not this year, not us, not—Christmas. Harold adored Christmasses, always. He was in his element, goodwill increased in him from the first of the month, the season vindicated his innocence, he seemed to go around wearing an invisible white woolly beard. But with the rest of the family, since they grew up, Christmas has been tricky. It has become my burden, wondering whether it would come off this year, if they would be willing to surrender to it, if I would, if it actually would happen or if we would just put on funny hats and exchange parcels and kisses and eat and drink and play a barren game together at playing a game that we used to play. And I, when I ought to go down on my knees with awe, am thinking about bread sauce and ten shillings for the postman, am remembering how marvellous they expect my Christmasses to be (this is one of the matriarchal legends they allow me to retain) and I must steer a difficult course between grown-up children who may snap and grandchildren who may be sick. I know that so much depends on me, I feel I am holding all their Christmasses in the palm of my hand, as if they had loaned me one of the great treasures of childhood.

And every year, no matter how uneasy I have been about it, there is a time when the blessing comes through the tinsel and outshines the fairy lights, and Christmas blazes down at us and we love each other fiercely, our closeness, our kinship. I don't know how we are going to do it this year.

And then, mercifully, a sore throat and a shivering body, and the doctor seated beside her on the bed, holding her wrist. She had enjoyed that, his solidity, the smell of the stuff of his suit, his weight altering her balance in the bed. This is one of the things you miss in widowhood, the casual acquaintance with another human body, not related in any way to passion but just the liberty of touching, being touched, of closeness and distance and their variations, the visible echo and evidence of your own presence.

" 'Flu," the doctor said. Julia overheard Liz giving the news to Sheena on the landing—Sheena didn't come in for fear of carrying infection to the children—"she'll be laid up over Christmas."

The pronouncement sounded like good tidings of great joy. Julia couldn't blame them—what a let-out for everyone! None of the seasonal attitudes were demanded, they could each make their own Christmas. Julia felt she had done the right thing. How kind, how fortunate to be excused.

And here a week before Christmas was Ralph, heavy with love and duty, bringing papers for her to sign from Mr. Edwards, the Solicitor. It was pleasant to have his company. She thought he seemed a little more self-conscious with her than usual, keeping an eye on himself in his mental mirror, but this was understandable, he was still shy of her widowhood, and perhaps also of his mother lying in bed with her hair fluffing round her face like an aged little girl. But she must not cheat by imagining her interpretation of him was correct—he was probably making a simultaneous appraisal of her. The gas fire and the carols going on further down the street (which didn't offend her now since they made no personal demands) provided a background for what he had to say.

Mr. Edwards had suggested that she should do this, do that. "Yes," she agreed, "yes," and signed where Ralph told her she should sign. Mr. Edwards wanted to know what she would like done about another matter. Ralph explained the alternatives. "Ask him what he thinks is best, dear." "He wanted to know what you thought." Doesn't he realise that I am excused from thinking, that with influenza added to bereavement I can lie here at Christmas and make no choices and no decisions? "What shall I tell him, Mother?" "What do you think would be best, Ralph?" You dodge widowhood a little by ignoring its responsibilities.

He sat on the low chair before the fire. In their physical attitudes and in some of their mannerisms, in their bulk shape Ralph and his father were alike. It might almost have been Harold. He sat with his feet apart, elbows on his knees and linked fingers, his hands swinging. He moved from business affairs to domestic ones, talking always into the pillars of the fire. She asked how his plans for Christmas were going, he said that everything was under control, he thought he had Christmas taped, he said.

"I suppose Sally-Anne is very excited."

"Well, I don't know; it isn't as if she was a child any more."

"Ralph, she's only thirteen."

"I know," he said, and she heard his fingers twisting, "but they grow up so quickly, these marvellous modern kids."

On both sides at once, she thought with amusement. You won't be able to keep that up for long. I know. I tried it. He told her that Sally-Anne wanted to give up ballet classes.

"I thought she was crazy about dancing."

"She's crazy all right, but not that kind of dancing any longer."

"What does her mother say?"

"Sal? She's all for it. She says the child isn't going to be a Sugar Plum Fairy indefinitely." She could see Sal saying it. He must have known this because he said quickly "Sal's dead right, of course. I see her point absolutely," giving his permission for his daughter to grow up and wiggle her hips.

Oh my poor Ralph. She asked him what he was giving

Sally-Anne for Christmas. A tape recorder, he said, pride and apology mixed. It was what she wanted.

"That will 'send' her, I suppose," Julia said. "Is that what they call a go present?"

He laughed unhappily. "They have a wonderful vocabulary, don't they? So vivid." She wished she didn't understand him so well and said it was a beautiful present and very generous, she was sure Sally-Anne would be delighted.

He said he thought she would and brightened.

"All the same I didn't know a child of that age would want a tape recorder."

"She'll be the first in her form to have one," he said.

"I see. What about Sal? Or is that a secret?"

He had chosen ear-rings for Sal. He hoped she would like them.

"Lucky Sal!"

"They're good ones," he said.

The carol singers had moved nearer. "In the Bleak Midwinter" came over clearly, with its substantial pathos of tenor backing. "Where's Liz?" he asked.

"Something at the church. I'm not sure."

"I ought to be going," he said and didn't move. The singers in the street had begun "O Little Town of Bethlehem". "You always liked that one, didn't you?" he asked, "it was one of your favourites."

Johnnie's radio asserted itself from the basement, tangling a modern beat with the carol.

"They're so dreary," she said, "the love songs nowadays. We used to enjoy being in love."

79

He came and stood beside the bed, foreshortened, with the bedside lamp making a caricature of his shadow against the wall. "Ah, but they've got something, the modern songs," he said painstakingly.

This irritated her and she challenged him. "What have they got, for instance?"

Her telephone took the opportunity to ring—how inanimate objects befriended her these days! Ralph stooped and this time kissed her cheek. "Get well soon and love from us all," he said, "I hope you'll have a restful Christmas," and left her, decently content with his performance.

"Restful." He had obviously worked on the word, writing alternative words on his blotting paper in the office, eliminating until he found one that was acceptable, honest but not extravagant. She was genuinely moved by this and felt tears falling on her fingers as she drew the receiver towards her.

"What is the matter?" Lionel asked.

"I am only crying a little because I have 'flu and I love my children very much."

"Two sensible reasons. How are you?"

"Better. Getting better."

"Has Madge been with you?"

"Madge? No. Why?"

"I only wondered. She didn't tell me she was going out tonight."

"My dear Lionel, do you have to issue your sister with an exeat?"

"Not quite," he said equably, "but she usually tells me and I just wondered. It isn't her Club Night."

"I'm sorry I can't help you."

"That's all right."

"How is Boy? Excited over Christmas, I suppose."

"He's certainly excited over something—being a bit awkward, they say at the Place. I suppose it's Christmas."

"And Isobel?"

"I have just had a card from her, so large it would hardly come through the door, with a picture of the angelic choir singing Gloria in Excelsis, and her best wishes in green ink." She heard him chuckling gently.

"Have you stopped crying?" he said, "that's good," and rang off.

Liz came in from whatever had been happening at the church. She brought Julia's hot milk and sat in front of the fire where Ralph had been sitting. The milk had slopped in the saucer, Julia emptied it back into the glass and hoped Liz didn't notice. Had it been a good evening, she asked. It depended, Liz said, on what you meant by good. How long was the Church going to go on pretending they knew all the answers? It made her mad. And the language. Inaccurate seventeenth century translations or Victorian sentiment. Later she relaxed and gabbled happily about nothing in particular. Julia felt the evening must have been good. And Sheena telephoned. It was probably chicken-pox, the puppy had chewed one of the vintage teddy-bears, and she must go now because the plum puddings were boiling dry.

Late in the evening Madge came. Julia heard her voice on the landing speaking to Liz and felt a stab of elation and curiosity. Madge had been staying away. Why? Which of them was supposed to have injured the other? It was gratifying that it had mattered to Madge. Sometimes Madge's devotion oppressed her, but tonight she was in the mood for it, to be loved unconditionally without having to apply the sliderule mathematics of family affection.

"Well, I don't know," Liz was saying, "it's late, isn't it? Wait and I'll ask." Then her head came round the door. "It's Madge, can she come in? I know it's late, and if you're tired—"

"Of course not. Come on Madge!" Liz withdrew, in silent disapproval. Madge had brought flowers from her garden, December jewels, Christmas roses, a spray of jasmin, viburnum fragrans, Garrya catkins not opened yet, and the early miniature yellow iris, Danfordia, she called it, with speckled tongues. "I coaxed them, they're early," Madge said of these. She laid them on the counterpane, touching them with her fingers as she named them.

"They're lovely. So fresh and beautiful." Come, love me, already I love your flowers.

"I thought you'd like them." Her eyes embraced Julia. Was it imagination or did her breath carry whisky with it?

"Lionel was on the phone earlier, asking whether you'd been here. He seemed a bit fussed and bothered."

Madge pushed her fingers through her hair. "Lionel? How idiotic!"

"He said you hadn't told him you'd be out. But that was ages ago. Where have you been?"

"Walking, walking."

"Why not the car, for heaven's sake?"

"I like walking." She shuffled off her stained sheepskin jacket which seemed stiff with night frost. She looked ill and tired, but had an air of purpose. So the flowers had not been enough, there was going to be a reconciliation scene.

"I know it's ages since I've been," Madge said, "donkey's ages." Her voice was a fraction too loud, too deliberate.

"Everyone's busy around Christmas. Anyhow I haven't been much in the mood for visitors."

"It was lousy of me to stay away."

Lousier to stand there at the bedside, draggled and exhausted and intense, accusing herself and making demands at this time of night. I can't bear dramatics but that's what she wants. Verbal extravagances. I wish she would go away.

"I've been thinking about what you said."

"Madge—"

"You were right of course, I should have seen it. If you want to talk about Harold—anything to do with Harold—then we should."

"Is that what you've come for?"

Apparently it was. Madge sat at the end of the bed and talked about Harold. She began at the beginning. Harold in sailor suits with the pockets bulging with marbles, Harold with bruised knees, Harold unhappy during his first terms at school, his letters home, Harold in the holidays bossy and unpleasantly assertive, Harold singing "O Faithful Fair One, O Fond and Rare One" rebelliously in his Mother's drawing-room for afternoon visitors—the scornful treble, the tinkle of the best china—Harold smoking secretly under the laurels behind the paddock, Harold, so brave, assuming responsibility when his father was killed, Harold at parties, always so reliable, so popular—Harold—Harold.

I know she is giving me something she values and thinks I ought to have, but I don't want it, and if she expects anything of the adult domestic Harold in return she will be disappointed. In any case I am not touched or stirred by these pictures of Harold's immaturity. They seem to me irrelevant and a little silly, I am only related to Harold as his wife. What she has told me is all very trite and unoriginal, a chapter from any Edwardian biography. Harold's childhood has no significance or value, I only acknowledge it grudgingly.

I made the mistake she is making when Ralph brought Sal home, I pretended to myself I was giving him to her, I was really staking my indisputable claim. I committed every foolishness, I told her what he had been like as a child, I repeated anecdotes, I brought out the photographs, the baby clothes, even the lock of hair. She looked past them and said "Oh yes," gently, and discarded them all. Nothing Madge can tell me about this boy she knew adds anything to my knowledge of my dead husband.

It had grown late, the street was almost empty of traffic, the carol singers had gone home. Johnnie's radio was silent. Liz called "Goodnight, Mother!" pointedly from the landing, waited for a moment and then went upstairs and banged her door. Madge was still talking about Harold with an eager monotonous appetite. Harold and summer tennis matches on damp grass courts—the ball has gone over into the kitchen garden, they are looking for it and taking their time and soon it will be too dark to play. The dusk aches, waiting for them.

84

Here Julia felt a prickle of interest. What had Harold been like with other girls? It was no use asking Madge, she didn't speak the language. Madge would have been keen to get back to the tennis. Harold, Madge said, Harold—Harold on cycling picnics, so amusing, Harold driving his first car, Harold studying for examinations, now on vacation from Cambridge, Harold skewered in a score of unfamiliar attitudes by her tenacious memory, now offered ceremonially. Harold—Harold—

The sacrifice wasn't yet complete. Madge had slipped on to her knees beside the bed, her arms spread across Julia's body. Her face was flushed. Repeatedly she put back wisps of hair that had fallen on her brow. She was still talking.

"And when he brought you home that first time we knew at once you were absolutely the right person for him. I remember how he looked at you."

And I remember how you looked at me, how you all looked, my glorious Harold's so glorious family, with polite anxiety and then with relief, approving my neat body and my ladylikeness, owning my body because it was to be owned by Harold, glad that I was pretty but not sexy, or if I was I looked the kind that could keep it to myself. I seemed, you told each other, a nice little thing. You wrote letters about me to outlying relatives. "Harold's Julia—we love her already."

"Everyone in Ireland thought Harold was so stiff when he came over for the wedding," she said, and watched Madge's astonishment.

"Stiff?"

"So English." She staked her right to childhood, fiercely, remembering Ireland, her own family, remembering how much of her Harold hadn't known, all he had robbed her of.

"Harold was never stiff. Never. Not—stiff."

"Of course when they got to know him—" she said, and Madge relaxed. She began to talk about Ralph, the expectant months. That shocking communal pregnancy, Julia thought, how did I get through it. Every one of his female relatives anticipated my conception, quickened, grew big with me.

The room was full of Madge's talk and the fire breathing. "And then you went back to Ireland for a holiday—."

"Not a holiday, Madge. It was my Mother. She died."

"I'd forgotten. So it was. So sad for you." Her condolences were perfunctory, Julia must have no roots except those that grew from Harold. "And when you came back and I saw you like that—I was so glad—so happy. It was wonderful." The memory that still fascinated and repelled jerked the words out of her. "As if it had been my child," she said.

She put her head down on her arms and wept, lying across Julia's knees. Julia stroked her hair, feeling choked.

"Don't cry. Please don't cry. You were wonderful to me. You've always been wonderful."

"Have I?"

Madge's body tightened. Julia said quickly "Wonderful to us all, you know we feel that."

Madge's breath was exhaled slowly, she grew slack and heavy. "Do you really feel that?"

"Of course we do."

This is a sad and silly scene. Madge raised herself kneeling upright, scrubbing her eyes. She took Julia's handkerchief when she offered it and began to clean up.

"Part of the family, we've always said so," Julia declared, adding a final idiocy.

Johnnie came in without knocking.

"I saw your light—" he said, and halted in the doorway. "What's up?" he accused, "what have you been doing to Madge?"

"Nothing, nothing."

"You have been doing something."

"Your Mother is very kind and I have been tiring her and I am an idiot," Madge said and heaved herself to her feet. "God how late it is, Julia, you should have thrown me out hours ago. Lionel will be running about the house like a sick hen, and the dog is on three-hourly pills."

"I'll take you home." Johnnie came round the bed and held her coat while she put it on.

"Oh will you, Johnnie? How kind."

"It runs in the family." He put an arm round her and they went off interlaced.

Julia lay back very tired and slightly indignant. Madge should have known better than to make a scene. How kind of Johnnie to take her home. It was a pity he hadn't remembered to bid his Mother goodnight.

Her head spun with Harold, boy and man, known and unknown. For a bright moment she desired and claimed and almost possessed him. Then turned to Ireland, to the nursery, to the womb.

87

CHAPTER SIX

She drew a deep breath, tightened her grasp on the door handle, and tried to shame herself by thinking of childbirth, the Bomb, the early Christian martyrs, then put her head round the kitchen door. "I'm just going out for an hour or so, Mrs. Parsons." The words having been released pursued each other mockingly round the walls. It was after lunch, the hour of the domestic doldrums. Mrs. Parsons was doing the brasses, achieving miracles with a fistful of blackened cloths. The kitchen reeked of Brasso, the shriven metal glowed palely. Every fortnight Mrs. Parsons did the brasses.

"Right-oh, then." Mrs. Parsons didn't lift her head or break the rhythm of the foot that kept time with the erotic beat from the kitchen radio.

Her indifference was an insult. It had taken Julia all morning to decide to go out and an hour to get dressed for the expedition. She had almost been defeated when she opened her wardrobe and was confronted by all those hats and coats. She would go back at once to the sofa and the television set. How could she be expected to choose or decide anything? This was the shape of the new lunacy that had taken hold of her. On the edge of any decision, no matter how trivial, her mind invented reasons against it. "Tea or coffee? Poached or boiled?" Liz asked in the morning. Even this was too difficult, the questions became issues and threatened her. The idea of any positive action filled her with nausea. She had been sick twice in the bathroom while deciding about a hat and coat. Come on, it's easy, nothing to it, take the dark green or the tweed. Instantly she was overcome with disgust for both of them, she couldn't reach her hand out to touch them, her organs shrank and curled. The blue then, what's wrong with the blue? She was paralysed with shame, remembering the last occasion when she had worn the blue. Black was right out of the question. In black one was either flaunting bereavement or looking smart, and in Julia's condition these were both serious social offences. For heaven's sake, don't stand there dithering like an idiot, what does it matter, who is going to notice you, a small unremarkable middle-aged woman setting off on an unnecessary errand. I know. I know. It never used to be like this. I chose things like a bird, I knew what was right, what was me. There was always a blessing on me when I was choosing, the things I ought to choose lay in wait for me and blossomed when I chose them. They were my justification. Go on then, take a hat and coat. I can't. I simply can not. I cannot bounce a ball in a vacuum.

In the end she closed her eyes, swearing a solemn and ridiculous oath to God that she would without delay take and wear the coat her fingers touched, and here she was at the kitchen door in pale beige and a cold sweat. It was a pity Mrs. Parsons was unmoved. I should have come down stark naked and saved myself a lot of trouble, Julia thought. That would have produced results. But the funny side of the predicament was itself alarming—if I can see how dotty I am being why can't I stop it? Am I suffering from the after-effects of 'flu or the after-effects of Harold, or have I just taken another step

89

in middle-age? I never really needed Harold to make up my mind for me, though sometimes I pretended I did. I am not released from anything by his death. There is no reason why I should feel so uncertain except that he isn't here to endorse my rightness.

The kitchen was the room that showed least evidence of Harold's absence. It was peaceable and orderly, kind predictable diligent Mrs. Parsons presiding. Perhaps she would go in and join her. Perhaps she would sit down at the other chair and ask to be given a cloth and Mrs. Parsons would pass articles of brass to her and tell her what to do and she would do it. Please, Mrs. Parsons. Let me come in. I will take off this hat and coat and you and I will be usefully employed together. "Picture of a Lady and a Woman cleaning Brasses"—a delightful domestic interior.

"Let me take a cloth, Mrs. Parsons."

"No sense in getting your hands messed up when you're going out."

The domestic interior should be styled "Two Ladies cleaning Brasses" Mrs. Parsons looked a lady this afternoon, her narrow face and long nose, the thick white eyelids, the ear-rings agitating with the ferocity of her polishing, all promoted her.

"How is Mr. Parsons keeping?"

Mrs. Parsons had been dull and uncommunicative about her husband recently. But now she smiled shyly and said "Coming on nicely, thank you." Julia envied her; so she was wooing him and didn't want to talk. What a pity. Oh to sit down and be drugged with Brasso fumes and scandalised by the story of Mr. Parsons' seduction!

She gave Mrs. Parsons the latest news of Sheena's new baby, prolonging it as much as she could.

"Taking your umbrella are you?"

"I suppose I might need it." There were only two umbrellas, it would be possible to swear another oath and do Eeny Meeny.

"Going to walk round the shops?"

"Yes." Yes, that was what she was going to do.

"Plenty of rubbish in the January Sales."

"I expect there is."

"I'll just close the door after me when I leave, shall I?"

Don't leave, alluring and ladylike Mrs. Parsons; there is no reason why either of us should leave. We will find so many brasses to clean that by the time we have finished the last of them the first will be ready for us again. There need be no end to it. I am frightened and unsure and indignant. I didn't expect to be like this when I was middle-aged. It isn't fair. By this time I should be poised and established, indelible and symbolic, like my Mother was, established in my mistaken rightness. But just now I came down the stairs and through the hall praying out loud and putting my feet down in the pattern demanded by childhood's bogeymen, touching the banisters in the way I must touch them if I am to avoid their fearful penalties. All those invented idiotic disciplines returned to me. I wonder how much sillier I can become and how long this is going on; it makes me very tired. I wish I were stretched out on a psychiatrist's couch in a tastefully-furnished room (velvet curtains in that dead divinely significant brown) spilling it all out to him, and the psychiatrist (such an intelligent face, such a gentleman) not at all surprised or offended by my story. This is another disturbing thought. I wonder if there is anything sexually sinister in the way I have begun to pine for a man. I just want a man to be near me. A man. Any man. I simply yearn for something male. The doctor sitting beside me on the bed, the solicitor bending down explaining about the money—even (oh torrent of warm shame) the postman, standing on the step in the clear air of a January morning, offering me a pencil to sign the registered packet. He was wearing mittens, there were strong hairs on the backs of his fingers, his nails were large and square. Desire for him poured over me, identifying itself with the bright frosty day. After he had gone I sat in the hall and trembled. I know I used sometimes to be a little arch with waiters and taximen who were too obliging (Harold bristled audibly), but this—! Will it get worse and shall I become an unpleasant old lady, so that they put me somewhere where the children can come on visiting days?

The telephone rang and she answered it. Mildred. Tomorrow was the wedding day.

"We're all going to miss you so much, Julia. I said to Daddy 'I simply must go and ring Julia and tell her how much we're all going to miss her'."

"That's very sweet of you, Mildred."

"I do wish you could have come."

So do I. Oh God so do I. How I would have loved it, the gay bright holiness of a wedding, the conventional tears and laughter, the slightly sexy fun (though I suppose these young moderns have seen the joke a long time ago so it wouldn't be so funny). Oh the joy of being wise and experienced and happy and charming, and the moment in the service when my heart turns over beyond all hope and belief and my eyes sting and I feel for Harold's hand—of course, I couldn't have gone. Liz was quite definite about it. "It's a pity," she said, "I suppose you'd have adored it. I can't think why—that one-day sanctity. The Church makes me sick the way they let people turn it into a social parade, all that money chucked around with half of the world starving."

Her diary this month was black with cancelled engagements —bridge, coffee parties, those literary evenings which were boring except for the interiors of other peoples' drawing-rooms and the interest of seeing Harold intriguingly different on his own wicket. "I don't know what I'm doing here," she used to say. "You supply the light and beauty," old Professor Blackett said. All these people reading through Thackeray and Smollett once every year—one wondered how they found the time to drink coffee and visit each other.

Julia asked Mildred how Wilfred was bearing up. It seemed that Daddy was running true to form. "He's so terrible when he's skittish, Julia. I bleed, I bleed." He had taken the bridesmaids to the pictures. The house of course was Bedlam. Cora was snappish. The bride was keeping calm.

"I'm sure she'll look simply lovely."

Mildred was sniffing. "They just don't realise, they're so young—when you think it's till death them do—oh my dear, whatever have I said?"

"Nothing, nothing."

"How wonderful you are, I shall tell Daddy."

She tried to retain the warmth of Mildred's voice as she left the house and made her way to the bus stop. She did not enjoy driving or being driven; the children drove too fast and too light-heartedly, Harold with a heavy dedication that made it impossible for his passengers to relax. When the children were driving her she prayed for survival and suffered, and hoped that they would not know. With Harold she implored Heaven that no idiot driver would cross his path. When Harold lost his temper and cursed they were both embarrassed and saddened, suffering a sense of loss like they did when he came into the bathroom while her squat pink body was still below the water. Poor Harold—but even the dear loves of tenacious romantics lose their waists, develop varicose veins and curved stomachs, dropped breasts and arches. So he cleaned his teeth noisily, keeping his back to her.

She was glad to find no one at the bus stop whom she knew. She climbed to the top deck and sat in the front, feeling a little giddy with her enterprise. She would ring Sal this evening on some pretext and let fall the information that she had been out—not making a thing of it, just a casual reference. And Liz. And Madge, of course. What pretty hair the conductor had, and long pointed suede shoes as if he were acting in a Shakespearian play. He called her "my love" in an affable offhand way. It was the first time since her encounter with the Hot Gospellers that she had met someone who knew nothing about Harold and made no adjustment to her. He chatted about his corns and his mother-in-law, both equally malevolent. His ordinariness was endearing. She felt exhilarated and stretched out her short legs, balancing herself by planting the toes of her shoes against the floor of the bus when it swayed on the corners. She felt gay and wished the ride were twice as long. She had been out already with Sal and Madge and Mildred on short conducted tours, like going about with a kindly warder. People they met asked "How are you?" as if they were signing a visitors' book, and went on to their own affairs quickly. She was much better on her own, unguarded and unobserved. Of course she was able to do it.

She would go first of all to the tea shop and have tea. But was that wise? It was the shop where all her friends went, already some of them would be there, chatty and hatted. Janice, who had spent the morning dusting her house, had turned the key and come confidently down town, knowing no dust would fall until she went back in the evening. Grace might be there with some of her cronies, holding a post mortem on a committee meeting, deciding what to leave out of the minutes. Julia didn't want to meet them, it would spoil her liberation and might not be fair to them. She imagined raised eyes, the flicker of embarrassment, the adjustment "Julia, my dear, what a nice surprise!" the concealed resentment at grief intruding on buttered tea cakes. What did one do about widowhood, anyway? There should be some established rules on how to be acceptably bereaved. Those of her friends who were widows had been awkward about it in a variety of ways. Maud, poor dear, one remembered what a dreary crêpe-ridden drag she had been and how hard they had tried to break through. "The Dance of the Seven Veils" someone had called it unkindly. And there was Hilary who couldn't stop talking, not about her dear dead Charles, but about what time she had got up and what she had done with herself during the morning, and what the dog had done, and what she had thought about, and what she had cooked for her lunch, and how, and what she planned to cook for her supper, as if these details only became real if she found an audience for them. And Janice—remember Janice?—you'd have thought it had been bubonic plague or something, the interior decorators had moved into the house almost as soon as the undertaker moved out, and she had bought new clothes and had a hair-do and thrown a terrific party, and the effort of being gay and natural had nearly slain them. And Ella had gone spiritualist and relayed dispatches from Ronald—one couldn't imagine a disembodied Harold getting chatty at a seance.

Julie knew by this time that her conduct wouldn't in any way measure the extent of her grief. She hadn't been able to measure it herself. She had tried. She thought about death deliberately, trying to assess it. She thought about her own death. She thought about the new carpet in the dining-room; the salesman said it would give her fifteen years. It was disconcerting to compete with a carpet.

She decided this afternoon to give her usual teashop a miss, so turned instead into a place she hadn't previously visited, a new place, these places sprang up overnight like mushrooms. Lighting in a variety of colours was squeezed from holes of uneven size and shape, cut in the ceiling. She wondered if the murals represented what one supposed them to represent. What in point of fact did one suppose—eyes or nipples, there really was, through lack of context, no way of being sure; they were certainly not navels, since they were distributed in pairs.

She sat at a table near the door, unhappily aware that she was a long, long way from home. The room was well filled with young men and girls who might have been creatures from another planet or straight out of an S.F. film. Meeting them in ones and twos on the pavement they would have been remarkable, a little absurd (you smile and say "these silly children" and feel better) but here they had authority. Their hair lay lankly as if they had just surfaced from a pool. There was nothing soft or pretty about the girls, no curve or cleavage, and though their legs were visible to the thigh the effect was surprisingly sexless. Their faces were bland as masks, eyes blackened, lips glossy and pale. For all their sophistication they had a look of arrested innocence. The men were more decorative, but sad-faded and a little pompous, like horses.

No tea, it seemed, but the waitress brought her coffee, black, slopped and already cool. She yearned for a tablecloth and paper napkins, china in the Indian Tree pattern, butter knives, twin sets and Jacqmar scarves. The poise of these children made her feel very lonely. They didn't appear to have taken any notice of her but she felt that already they had labelled her as some kind of a freak, and were hostile. Her pale beige coat and hat, her plain court shoes, became laughable, antiquated fancy dress. Her gloves and handbag were amusing oddities. The children leaned against each other or sat interlocked, gazing into each others' faces. There was no sign of joy, no passion, only a delicate and dedicated involvement. Some of the girls stroked and petted. The boys sprawled, indifferent and godlike.

She was frightened of them. She remembered nostalgically

97

a variety of young men who had sat at the other side of the table from her in a variety of cafés, their Anzora-smooth hair, their dark suits, her crêpe de chine blouse with the string of small pearls, fingers brushing as cups were passed, the bleating violin half hidden behind palms. They had been killed in the war, shot or burned, drowned or wasted in prisons, or else they were old men now, or had lately died, like Harold. She had no right to be here.

A man came in and stood for a moment, then asked her if he could sit at her table. She nodded permission. He thanked her; it was the only empty seat, he said. She praised God silently that it was the only empty seat. He was a soft, heavily-built, florid man of about forty, a commercial traveller, she guessed, but he was a creature of her own species. She smiled an extravagant welcome. He said he hadn't known it was this sort of a place, he wasn't familiar with the city. When his coffee came he sent it back, stating that it was cold. The waitress, like a medieval pageboy in tights and tabard, slopping in sandals and with her hair tied up in a flowered dish cloth, looked startled, then brought him another cup and set it down with studied nonchalance. If she had had a bottom worth his attention Julia felt sure that this man would have slapped it, but she seemed anatomically disappointing.

"These kids, look at them," the man said, deeply melancholic. "I ask you."

Oh splendid man. Julia felt herself bloom. "You have to forgive them," she said, being self-trained in automatic tolerance. He said he didn't see why. She sipped her coffee. "The

Mushroom Cloud; they have had to grow up in the shadow of it."

"Do you know what I grew up with?" he said. "Well, I'll tell you. Eternal damnation, everlasting torment, that was my little lot. Writhing in the fire that is not quenched under the eye of a Merciful Creator. We believed it. Being blown to bits by an atom bomb would have been a kindness. These kids have got rid of hell and sin. I don't think they're doing too badly."

"Do you believe in hell? I mean—now?"

The man gave her a look of uneasy honesty. "I hadn't much choice. I married into the Brethren."

"I see."

"She's dead now."

"I'm sorry."

"She has gone to her reward," he brooded, staring at his hands on the plastic table-top, thinking of the girls. His hands were thick-fingered and plump. Julia experienced a keen desire to cover them with her own, to hold her hands there, to see what reaction this produced in him and among the children at the other tables. Would it, between people of her generation, seem an obscene gesture? It was tempting to try it out. But she restrained herself, there was a look in the man's eyes that suggested he had guessed. So she paid her bill and bade him good-day, and left, feeling elated.

As she made her way to the shops her instinct told her that she had picked her day well. The busy scented air stirred in her the familiar appetite. On all sides of her articles were massed which would make life easier, warmer, softer, more gracious,

99

more colourful, more congenial. Their variety amazed her. If she bought them and took them home they would become constant predictable friends. Or she could wander here for ever, allowing herself to be delighted by them.

She decided to buy, and was charmed by the ease with which she did it. It was simple. Joyfully and precisely she made her selection. One of those, no, make it two, there is twice the security in having two. And four of those, why not, they will be an insurance against the future. Everything she bought enchanted her. She bought this, and this, and this. She became as charming as the objects she bought presupposed that she must be. The girls behind the counter were all very kind, she felt they must realise how much this meant to her. And if in the excitement she muddled her money or left her glasses behind or forgot to pick up the parcel from the counter they put her right affectionately. She became dizzy with success and bought and continued to buy. Look, I can do it, watch me choosing, the spell is broken, the bogeymen are all dead—and I'll take a dozen and a half of these.

The assistants smiled their applause, the act of buying and selling had became a mutual compliment. Three pairs of those, yes, three, they will lie in the drawer in their plastic packets and next time I am unhappy or lonely or confused I will open the drawer and take them out and count them and be comforted. One could see Madam had an eye for nice things, they said, quality told. Madam had always had an eye. My glasses again! How kind and clever of you to remind me! And how deliciously absurd of me!

She had forgotten that it could be like this, she had been out in the cold so long. She knew now what she could do with her afternoons, with her mornings too, perhaps. There was a physical joy in spending money. Sometimes her purchases were a little mad but with a gay madness that was itself a kind of wisdom. She bought three woolly turbans like tea-cosies in three different shades, giggling a little because they were all so pretty and silly and because life would be very entertaining with three woolly turbans. She felt as exhilarated and exhausted as if she had spent the afternoon giving birth, or in bed with a lover.

"We're closing, Madam," the assistants said gently. It was just as well, she was tiring and her purse would soon be empty. Where was her purse? Somewhere at the bottom of her handbag, of course, this bag was inconveniently deep. She pawed and dredged among lipsticks, nail-files, library tickets, combs, but found no purse. Don't panic, it was there a moment ago, you will find it as soon as you put on your glasses. Where were her glasses? Bag and pockets yielded no glasses.

"We're just closing," the assistants said a little more emphatically. The loops of string on her fingers tangled and shackled her. Surely there should be five loops and there were only three. And the umbrella—dimly she remembered that at one time there had been an umbrella. Alarm and confusion increased.

They were spreading white cloths along the counters. "We're closing," they said impatiently. Lipstick and pen had rolled out of her bag and were on the floor. She stooped to recover them, a stocking tightened and zipped up her knee.

Her hands were immobilised with parcels. Gloves? Where were her gloves?

Her head spun. It was all too difficult. She was not seeing anything very distinctly. Some of the lights had been turned off, the aisles between the counters had emptied. The assistants' faces came and went inexplicably, like waxing and waning moons. The floor was rising gently and sinking again. She found a chair and sat down and began to weep.

The moons steadied and converged. "Has Madam lost something?" Shame poured over her head.

My purse, she intended to say. My purse, my gloves, my glasses and some of my hairpins, a few parcels, my wits, my dignity, my lovely afternoon. Instead she heard herself saying "My husband!" and knew that she was making an exhibition of herself, sitting in a public place among strangers, bawling for Harold, hearing herself and being unable to stop.

They were very kind and helpful. They found her handkerchief, her glasses, her parcels, her purse and her umbrella. They also found a taxi and steered her into it. She sat in the back seat afraid to move for fear any of her possessions would take flight again and wept cautiously.

She was still weeping when she reached the house and paid for the taxi. "All right then, are you?" the man asked awkwardly. "Perfectly all right," she sobbed and he slid the money into his pocket and drove away quickly.

She prayed that her key would be there and it was, but her hand shook too much to allow her to fit it into the lock. Someone was crossing the gravel. Oh for a secret place into which she could creep quietly and be private. What would Liz say, or Johnnie? The key still evaded the keyhole; life was too difficult and too unkind, and all inanimate objects were her enemy.

"I can help, perhaps?"

Not Liz. Not Johnnie. It took her a moment to recognise Max, Johnnie's Nigerian friend, the one who composed music. In the half light he seemed faceless, the street light only lit up his eyes and his teeth. He took the key from her and put it in the lock and turned it. "Wait a moment and I will put on the light for you," he said and did so. The light revealed a dishevelled, tear-streaked silly old woman. "The mother of Johnnie," he said, identifying her.

"Is Johnnie home?"

"Not yet. I am waiting. Soon he will come."

His voice was soft, lacking rhythm and emphasis. She began to disentangle the parcels from her fingers, the strings had twisted and were hurting. He helped her to free herself. "You have been distressed," he said.

"I went out shopping by myself and I cried in the shop. '

"Why not?" he said. "You are a good woman, my Mother cried in all the shops. In the shops and at home she cried."

Thank you. How kind you are to tell me this. I imagine a peasant woman in a shanty in darkest Africa weeping into her cooking pots; that is nonsense, your Mother probably lives in a sophisticated flat and weeps into the latest labour-saving devices. But I am glad you told me. None of the children could talk to me like this. When we try to talk we suspect each other of insincerities and extravagances, so that the truth which is the valuable thing is damaged.

"Come in," she said, "I'll make a cup of tea while you're waiting for Johnnie."

"It would give you trouble."

"It would give me pleasure."

She led the way into the kitchen and filled the kettle while Max found cups and milk and sugar. Everything he did was quiet and easy. His dark skin against her patterned china fascinated her. She made the tea and poured it, and they sat at either side of the kitchen table.

He stirred his cup, watching her. She sipped her tea, feeling relaxed and comforted. "How is your Mother now?"

"She will never be the same."

"I'm sorry."

"Don't be sorry," he said, "one doesn't expect to be the same."

She set her cup down. "What does one expect? That's what I'd like to know."

He lifted his shoulders in a liquid shrug, expressing infinite compassion.

"But I'm getting better," she said. "This afternoon I went out shopping by myself. Look at all the things I bought."

"So many many parcels!"

"This," she said, "isn't it pretty? And this!" She pulled out scarves, blouses, handkerchiefs, cosmetics, stockings. "This and this and these!" She heaped them up on the table.

"Like Christmas come again," he praised. He lifted one of the scarves, admiring its brilliance, and held it extended on the splayed pink tips of his fingers.

"And everyone was so kind. And I bought these—just look

at these!" The woolly hats, three variations of the same joke. She twirled them on her hands, laughing. "Do you like them?"

Max liked them very much. He chose the liveliest of them and put it on his head and she applauded and chose another for herself. He got up and went to look at his reflection in the mirror, adjusted the headgear to a different angle and came back across the tiled floor with his feet moving in a stuttering shuffle while he beat out a rhythm with his palms against his thighs.

"Oh wonderful!" she cried. It was all so unexpectedly amusing. She rose and approached him, arms on hips, tango-fashion, tapping her heels.

It was at this moment that Liz and Johnnie came in and stood in the doorway, gaping. How alike they were with their faces stiffened in critical amazement.

"Mother!"

"What on earth is going on?"

Max had snatched the hat off his head and was twisting it between his fingers. He threw it down among the rest of the stuff.

Liz pointed at the rainbow heap. "What have you been doing? What are all these things? Is it a bazaar or something?"

"I've been out," she snapped.

"By yourself?"

"I am still capable of finding my way around."

"You could have asked Madge or Mildred—"

"I didn't. I went shopping and bought one or two things."

"One or two—!"

"I had a splendid time. Everyone was so kind. I had tea in

a new place, very entertaining. And I met a most interesting man. We had quite a talk."

"A man!" Liz's face was amusing but it annoyed her.

"A man, dear. You must know. An adult male. We shared a table."

"Who was he?"

"I told you. I met him. A Commercial, I should think."

"You mean a pick-up? How could you?" Liz's voice rose to a squawk. "What did you talk about?"

"Hell and the Bomb and sex. He had original views."

"Mother!"

"If you could see yourselves—" Julia giggled.

"How did you get all this stuff home?"

"In a taxi. They put me in a taxi."

"They?"

"The women in the shop. I was tired and a little confused. They were very kind."

"You aren't ill, are you?"

"I told you. I was just a little upset."

They stared, trying not to feel sorry for her.

"All right," she said, "I'll tell you. I lost things. I behaved like an old woman. I howled."

"Mother!"

"I'm sorry, Liz."

But their sympathy was exhausted. "What shop was it?" Liz demanded. "I'll never go there again. I couldn't."

Johnnie said: "Oh for any sake, Liz. Come on, Max, if you're coming."

CHAPTER SEVEN

So Gran was coming to stay. It happened suddenly. Halfway through Juke Box Jury the telephone rang, and Mum, who didn't like Juke Box Jury and always sat looking the other way till it was finished said "I'll take it, Ralph." There was a man on the panel who was dreamy, much better than David Jacobs and not nearly so old. She wished she could be one of the audience; she knew exactly what she would do to her hair, what expression she would wear when the camera picked her out. She had practised it. Later in the programme the camera would come back to look for her. "There's that interesting girl again," people said, "such an unusual face. I wonder who she is."

"What d'you think of that one, Poppet?" Dad asked "Hit or Miss—come on, tell us, you're the expert." He always tried very hard to be interested. And then Mum came in and her face was different and Dad said "Is there anything wrong, sweetheart?"

Mum said it depended what you meant by wrong, and Dad said: "Let's have it." So she sat beside him on the sofa. Sally-Anne couldn't decide whether to go on listening to the telly or to try and hear what they were saying; she knew by their voices that they thought she wasn't listening.

Mum said that was Liz on the telephone. Liz said to tell Dad that something would have to be done about Mother. Dad said wasn't it anything Liz could do, and Mum said he knew what Liz was like when she was in one of her states, and Dad said Liz had been absolutely wonderful about everything, and Mum said "Yes, I know. But I think she's had enough. Ralph, I never thought your Mother would have been like this," and Dad said "I don't know what you mean," and Mum looked at him sideways and changed whatever it was she had been going to say, and just said "Oh, nothing."

Then Dad asked "What about Sheena? Can't she do anything? Did Liz say if she'd got on to her?"

"Sheena? The way she's fixed?"

"I'd forgotten."

Mum laughed and said: "I don't know how you could; it's a permanent thing with Sheena."

Dad laughed too, not a very good one and said "Sheena and her brood, they're marvellous!" and Mum didn't say anything, just sucked in the sides of her mouth and smoothed her skirt. Then she noticed that Sally-Anne was listening and she said "Gran's coming to stay," and looked across at Dad, smiling. And then it was the end of the programme and the panel were laughing and talking to each other, pretending they didn't know that their names were running across their faces. It must be bliss to have your name running across your face like that and pretend you don't know.

In bed she lay awake for ages and ages, staring at her private landscape on the ceiling, the dark cliff of the wardrobe, the mirror's icy pool, the dim faces of her pin-ups, and the way the light from the street changed the pattern on the curtains into forest trees. She ached for them to come upstairs. Miles away she heard the comfortable sound of their voices; they were not laughing very much tonight. She said Our Father again, hoping that perhaps God would be some good but He wasn't. She felt frantic with loneliness. She wondered what they would say if she pranced downstairs in her pyjamas and told them: "Talk to me now. It's my turn."

Every quarter of an hour the clock in the hall chimed, reminding her she was still awake. It made fun of her. Why don't you sleep with your door shut, Sally-Anne, a big girl like you? Are you afraid of something? Will you still be awake next time I chime? It's getting very late, later and lonelier. Do you think they have forgotten to come upstairs? Perhaps they won't ever come. Can you hear them any more?

At last, ages and ages afterwards, the door downstairs opened and they were coming. Their voices were polite, not lazy and loving like sometimes. Mum said it would be better if she moved her things out of the spare room wardrobe tonight and Dad said much better leave it till tomorrow she was tired now, come on to bed, but Mum said there would be plenty to do tomorrow, she would do it now. And so she did it, running backwards and forwards across the landing, with her heels tap-tapping.

"Everything I possess will be madly crushed of course," she said, and Dad said "She's my Mother after all, Sal. We must do what we can," and Mum said "Of course, darling, that's what we're doing, isn't it?"

Ages and ages afterwards Mum came in. She had been having her bath, she smelt sweet and flowery, and the silk of her dressing-gown creaked. "Still awake? You should have been sleeping hours ago. Did I make too much noise getting ready for Gran? Poor Gran is very unhappy, and we must all be very kind to her when she comes, mustn't we?"

Dad called "Sal!" from across the landing, and Mum called back: "In a minute, Ralph!" softly.

"Isn't Dad coming in, Mum?"

"I'm sure he is."

"Come on. Bed's lovely," Dad called.

Mum went to the door and said in a scolding whisper "The Infant, Ralph, she says you didn't come in to see her."

"Oh God," Dad said, and Mum kissed her and went away.

Then Dad came. His dear and beautiful shadow, like a blessing, travelled over the carpet and then over the mat and then reached the bed and fell on her. This was the loveliest thing that happened. But tonight she made herself stiff and didn't reach out.

"Did you forget about me, Dad?"

"Of course I didn't. I was just keeping it to the last." His voice matched the darkness. She snatched out for him and held him close. Through his pyjama jacket she could hear his heart bumping black lies but she didn't care.

She put her hand to his cheek and ran her finger slowly along her favourite channel. "What'll we talk about, Dad?"

Mum called "Don't keep the child awake, Ralph!" and she knew it was spoilt. She twined her arms round his neck but he wasn't thinking about her.

"Too late for talk, Poppet, and Gran's coming tomorrow. We must all be very kind to Gran, mustn't we?"

"I know."

To pay him back she let her mouth go soft and open when he kissed her, pressing up against him and rubbing, the way they did it on the telly, because she knew he didn't like it. He took his mouth away at once, and kissed her forehead, like a hen pecking, and went away, and when the light on the landing had gone out and their door was closed she put her head below the bedclothes and made rude noises and cried a bit and was asleep before the clock chimed again.

So next day Gran came. She didn't like Gran very much. She was old and she had a way of looking at you as if she knew things about you, secret things, that she couldn't possibly have known. Her neck was stringy. The things she said weren't interesting or funny and you found yourself thinking about the things you said instead of just saying them. And you must be sorry for her because she was unhappy but this was too frightening and unfair to think about. Grown up people had no right to be unhappy. Anyway, what was she unhappy about?

There was a Bible with a marker in it on the table beside Gran's bed in the spare room, and one night when Sally-Anne was going across the landing to the loo because this sometimes helped with going to sleep, Gran's door was open and there was Gran saying her prayers and looking peaceful and happy. So if she was sure Grandpa had gone to heaven then that was all right, wasn't it? Gran would soon be in heaven herself. She wished she could be religious like Gran. She would show them all how religious she could be. But Mum would only think she was off her nut, and any time she'd asked Dad about God and things like that he rubbed his nose and said "Listen,

Poppet, there are some things that are hard to understand until you're older and it's a pity to get hold of the wrong end of the stick. So let's leave it in the meantime and later on you can make your own mind up—eh? Just you be a good girl and love Mummy and Dad and be kind to other people, and if anything bothers you you come and ask me and I'll explain it for you—how's that?" He put his finger below her chin when he said that, and tilted her head back, looking at her so beautifully that it was very nearly all right. But all the same it must be super to be religious, like Gran.

Perhaps Gran was just pretending. People pretended a lot. You knew when they were doing it, and you paid them back by pretending to them. So that when a play on the telly turned sexy in the middle and Dad sat up and said "This is all rather silly, isn't it? We don't want to watch such boring rubbish, do we, Poppet?" and switched off, you put stars in your eyes just to spite him and wriggled a little and said "Oh, but Dad I thought it was simply super," and this made him much more worried than if you'd just got up and stamped out of the room with a red face like a kid and banged the door. You loved him very much and it served him right for pretending, but it was interesting to know you could do this to him—Dad was scared stiff of sex as well as religion—and you wondered what else you could do, and you knew Mum wasn't the only one who could do things to him.

When Gran came to stay life was muddling because everyone was always changing sides. Perhaps it was worst for Dad because sometimes he had to be on Gran's side. Or worst for Mum, being on the other side? Or for her because Dad seemed so much smaller and ordinary? Nothing was the same when Gran came to stay. Everyone tried very hard. It was very tiring, as if you were out visiting all the time. And you never knew what little thing was going to be important and terrible.

"I've been admiring your ear-rings," Gran said. "Ralph let me into the secret before Christmas. I think they're charming."

"They are nice, aren't they?" Mum put up her fingers and stroked the ear-rings. Her nails were done with the mother-of-pearl paint. She looked very pretty. Some girls' Mums were simply frightful. All the girls at school thought that Mum was gorgeous.

"He told me they were something rather special," Gran said. "May I see?"

Mum unhooked one of the ear-rings and gave it to Gran to hold. Gran put on her glasses to see it better. She held it up to the light, carefully, because it was rare and precious. It swung. "Yes, how clever of him," Gran said, "Ralph has always had a flair for choosing the right thing. I wonder where he got them. Are you going to inherit your father's taste, child?"

Then Mum said "I suppose I may as well tell you, this isn't the pair Ralph chose, I changed them."

"You—?"

"Oh he didn't mind at all, you know how sweet he is, so long as I got what I wanted that was all right. The pair he'd chosen—if you'd seen them, Mamma, you'd have known. I just couldn't pretend they were me. So of course I had to tell him and he said go ahead, change them, get something you want. And I did."

"I see," Gran said, and gave the ear-ring back to Mum as if she'd been handing her a penny for the loo. Mum put it back in her ear without looking at Gran. Then, with her back to Gran, Mum said: "It's no good pretending things are any better than they are, is it?" And when Gran didn't answer Mum said "I try. I do try." Then Gran grabbed hold of Sally-Anne and smoothed her fringe back from her eyes so that she knew she must be looking hideous. Gran stared at her, there were little threads on the white parts of Gran's eyes. Gran said: "The child has such a good brow, Sal, it seems a pity to hide it," and held her close against her for a minute, as if she was picking her for her side.

On Sunday Gran asked whether she would like to come to church with her, and Mum and Dad didn't say anything, so she said she would. She liked church. She was wearing her best coat. There was a boy sitting near who kept looking at her, she wondered if Gran noticed. The hymns were lovely. Gran sang them all in a sharp shaky voice without needing to look at the hymnbook. When everyone stood up and said solemnly "I Believe" it was very beautiful. She felt smoothed out and good, sitting in the pew beside Gran. The boy kept on looking at her during the sermon.

Dad said: "How did it go, Poppet?" and Mum looked up to see, so she said "I suppose it was all right. The hymns had awfully crumby words, some of them were real slop," and Dad smiled privately and she daren't look at Gran's face and hated herself with a black disgust and hated them for making her be like this.

That night she stayed awake till half past two, which was a

record. She was very frightened and miserable and began to cry on purpose, a little louder than usual, in the hope that someone would be awake and would hear. Gran came in. Her dressing-gown was thick and woolly.

"What is it dear? Having a bad dream?"

"I'm not sure. Did I wake you up?"

"I wasn't sleeping."

Gran patted her hand and sat at the bottom of the bed with a rug wrapped round her. The street lights made her look like a little hunched-up sheep. Several times she seemed to be going to say something but in the end she said nothing at all. Her head nodded and there was a light snore.

After a while the clock struck three and Gran's head came up and she said "Feeling better now, are you?" and she went off. Sally-Anne didn't hear the clock again until the morning.

Next day Mum said "What's this about you having nightmares?" and she said "Don't fuss, Mum, it was quite all right. Gran came in."

She drew out some of her savings from the post office without telling and bought extra sweets and ate them in secret. She got spots and headaches and had to stay off school because her eyes went fluttery in art class. It was cold outside, there were frost pictures on the windows every morning. Gran and Mum were always having an argument about whether Gran was cold. Gran wore three cardigans and said she was warm as toast. She said she wouldn't sit in Dad's chair and then she sat in it, so that the family pattern was spoilt.

On Saturday afternoon it was sunny and Mum said "Gran's going to be an angel and take Punch across the park for his walk. What about you going with her, dear, it would be company and do you good," and Dad said "That's right, Poppet. Breath of fresh air is what you need."

"No. No, please."

"Oh come on," they coaxed, "you can't go on being an invalid for much longer."

"Gran would like it—wouldn't you, Gran?"

She had already made plans for the afternoon. It was going to be lovely, the way she had arranged it. The film was a Western. She would suck sweets and goggle and get herself into a lovely woolly daze and be excused from everything that was going on. In a Western nobody changed sides, nothing was complicated. There were Goodies and Baddies and a Happy Ending.

Mum said: "It's the wretched telly, that's what it is. The child is an addict, Ralph," and Dad said "You can't clamp down on it altogether if the other kids are allowed to watch—" and Mum said that wasn't the point.

"Is it the telly, Poppet?"

"No. No of course not."

So they decided she was to go with Gran. Mum and Dad came to the door and waved goodbye and went inside smiling.

Punch pranced and pulled on the leash and his breath made white smoke. Gran's face was small and grey and she'd put her lipstick on wrong, like she nearly always did. She panted when large dogs came and sniffed at Punch, so that you knew she was frightened. "I hope he won't fight," she fussed, tugging. Sally-Anne remembered Mum and Dad at home, she thought of the graceful cowboys, the horses wheeling, the pursuit, the beautiful righteousness of the happy ending, the bliss of being excused. "He's a terrible fighter when he starts," she lied, and wondered how long unhappiness like this could go on.

In the park they met Cousin Lionel and Boy. Boy was bouncing a ball on a piece of elastic. If his hair was longer he'd look quite dreamy; it was a pity he was a bit batty but it made him interesting, something to tell the other girls.

"Lionel!" Gran cried, looking up at him as if he was John Lennon. At once she got quite pink and lively.

Cousin Lionel said: "What are you doing, Julia?"

"Surely you can see, I am being usefully employed. We are all exercising each other, the child and the dog and I. The house is taking a rest from us. I do the flowers and the library books and some of the messages as well, it's a full life. Why hasn't Madge been round to see me? She knows where I am."

"You ask her."

Gran said: "Lionel. What is it about Madge?"

Cousin Lionel took his glasses off and polished them—he looked quite different—and said: "I wouldn't pay too much attention to Madge," and put his glasses on again.

Gran said: "Of course you wouldn't tell me; you were always on Madge's side. Anyway, tell her from me she was right, will you?"

"Right? About what?"

"She said 'You have the children'. So I have. Or rather, they have me."

"Is that what you want?"

"I don't want anything very much. I made a mess of it on

117

my own anyway. I was a fool to try. I suppose they told you, it was very funny, you'd have thought it was."

Cousin Lionel skewered the point of his stick into the icy puddles on the path and said "Julia, Julia," in an unhappy kind of way, not looking at Gran. Then he said "You're an idiot, Julia, you should have been able to make a better job of things," and Gran said "I know. Only I didn't think it would be like this," and blew her nose, and Cousin Lionel snorted and poked a loose piece of ice angrily out of the puddle and whacked at it with his stick, and Punch went crazy trying to chase it, so that Gran almost fell over and the leash slid out of her hand, and he was away over the grass like a streak, trailing the leash behind him.

"Oh Lionel!" Gran wailed, clasping her hands. She looked scared, as if it was the crack of doom. "Lionel, he's gone! What am I going to do!"

Cousin Lionel said: "For God's sake Julia pull yourself to-gether. The children will soon bring him back." Punch had almost reached the thick bushes on the far side of the grass and was still going. "Run!" cried Cousin Lionel, flapping his hands as if he was shooing hens, "get him!"

"Chase, chase!" Boy shouted. Suddenly she was running. It was like being let out of prison. She had forgotten what being happy was like.

The grass was crisp and springy with frost, the air rushed past them, her hair blew back, her ears throbbed and stung. "Chase, chase!" Boy cried, whooping and prancing. He looked a sight, but she didn't care. She didn't care about anything. She ran, leaving them all behind, the people, the arguments, all the sour tired difficult things. She ran and ran. "Chase!" Boy cried.

The winter sun, coming like spears of yellow light through the clouds, coloured their faces and bodies and dazzled their eyes. It seemed solid so that they had to push their way through the air. Boy reached his hand out and she took it and they ran together. Now they had come to the long shadows of the bushes, now to the bushes themselves; a cloud of small dark birds rose out of them and up into the air, whirling and whirling. The sun painted their wings as they climbed. There was no sign anywhere of Punch. She called and called and her voice came back to her empty.

"Chase!" Boy still cried.

She turned to look back. Gran and Cousin Lionel were a long way off, two strangers, a little old lady and gentleman who didn't matter.

Boy said: "Ducks! Lake!" and pointed. The path to the lake led through bushes which made a tunnel. It was dark going through them, they were so thick that the sunlight was shut out. The lake when they reached it was quiet and very beautiful, a secret place, frozen over from edge to edge, like black glass. At one end you could hear water running below the ice like a voice talking and talking, a long way off. Some of the long overhanging branches had been held fast in the ice.

Ducks came squawking from the other side of the lake. The clatter of their wings frightened her. "Funny ducks!" Boy said. They alighted on the ice some yards off on clumsy pink feet, and slid the rest of the way, sending up fountains of dry frost.

Boy laughed and jumped and clapped his hands. He

hunted below the bushes for loose stones and threw them at the ducks who panicked and fought in their effort to get away. Some of their feathers were loosened and lay on the ice.

"Don't!"

But he went to fetch more stones. The ducks rose on their toes and stretched out their necks and thrashed the air with their wings, looking silly, and then became beautiful as the air lifted them. The commotion stirred the loosened feathers and let them fall as the ducks made their escape.

He went in search of heavier stones, wrenching them out from among the stiff knotted roots of the bank. How strong he was! He held the stones up in both hands and let them come crashing down on the lake's edge and shouted as they fell. The ice splintered whitely and cracked, and a skin of water ran out over it slowly, with a sucking noise.

He went out on the ice, and when she didn't follow said: "Cowardy cowardy!" He jumped up and down, the ice whined and seemed to tilt. He pulled up a frozen stick and beat the ice with it. He hit at the drifting feathers.

"Suppose they're coming to look for us," she said, and ran up the path. Yes, they were coming. Halfway across the grass were two small gilded figures, moving slowly. Gran was holding on to Cousin Lionel's arm, you could tell by the way she was walking that her shoes were hurting.

She sped down the path again and reached the lake. "They're coming!"

Boy laughed and said "Hide! Boy hide!" He took hold of her arm and pulled her with him into a deep bush. Twigs caught at her hair and whipped her face.

He was hurting her arm. He kept on hurting it while Cousin Lionel's shoes and Gran's shoes came up the path close beside them. The shoes stopped. Gran was panting.

"The animal will find his own way home," Cousin Lionel said. "It must have that much sense. And if it can, the children can."

Gran said: "I can't go back without the child. I can't."

"Are you frightened of them?"

"Yes."

"Properly in their clutches, aren't you?"

"I told you, Lionel, I must have someone."

"What is she? A shrew or a bitch or a bit of both?"

"They are dear sweet children, but I am sick and tired of trying to give satisfaction."

"If you could settle for being thoroughly unpopular, Julia, you'd have a much easier time. But you always had to be liked."

"O God, Lionel," Gran said, "what can have happened to the girl?"

"Nothing from Boy, if that's what you mean. Look, I'll come back to the house with you. They'll be there before us."

"O Lionel, do you think so?"

The shoes turned and went back the way they had come. Boy let go of her arm and they came out from the bush.

"Ha ha! Hee hee!" Boy said, making rude faces in the direction that Gran and Cousin Lionel had gone. She taught him some he didn't know. It didn't take him long to learn.

They ran along the edge of the lake and reached its farthest point. They had come clear of the bushes now. The sun was so low that its light seemed to be lying flat along the top of the winter flower beds. It made the floor of the bandstand golden. All the air was golden.

Boy jumped up on the bandstand and spun round and round, whooping, with his hands spread out.

"Show off!" she jeered. "Baby show off!"

He said: "Boy dance!" He pranced about and kicked. "Dance!" he ordered her.

She climbed up beside him and began to dance, choosing a Scottish reel. The sun had gone now, there was only a yellow stain left in the sky and it was colder. She felt tired. Boy didn't seem to know even the easier steps. He wasn't trying.

She stopped dancing. "You're spoiling it!"

He went on hopping and kicking, shouting "Boy dance!"

She stamped and shouted at him: "I think you're silly, that's what I think!"

Terrifyingly he began to cry out loud, rubbing his knuckles into his eyes. And then the first stroke of the bell at the park gate rang out.

"Quick!" she cried, "they're closing the gates, we'll be shut in!"

But he wouldn't stop crying and when she pulled him he kicked at her like a baby. Once he caught her wrist and she thought he was going to hit her. "Oh hurry! It's a long way back!" All the time the bell was ringing, and it was growing colder and darker.

"All right," she said, "I'm going if you're not!" She twisted free from him and plunged again into the dark path that skirted the lakeside. It was pitchy black. After a while she thought she could hear him running behind her but she didn't turn or slacken pace. He was still crying. The bell was still ringing, she waited for every stroke.

Just before she reached the grass he caught up with her. "Hurry! There's still time!"

She snatched his hand and they began to cross the grass in the direction of the gate. It seemed a long, long way. The houses on the road that ran beside the park railings had lighted windows, the lights of cars slid along the road.

Now their feet were on the gravel driveway. She could see the skeleton shape of the gate making stripes across it. A man was standing beside the gate, it was almost closed. He shouted something after them as they ran through but they didn't stop. Now their feet struck the pavement, headlights shone on them.

She stopped at last to get back her breath. Boy had no handkerchief, she lent him hers. He seemed dismal and frightened. "Home now," she said. To cheer him up she put pennies in a slot machine outside the shop at the corner, and got some bubble gum and gave it to him, and he made comforted noises and came a little quicker.

They turned the last corner, they saw the lights of home. Punch barked as they came up the drive. The door opened before they had reached the porch. They came in hand in hand. "We're back!" she announced.

They were all in the hall, Mum, Dad, Cousin Lionel, Gran. They stood with their mouths open, looking silly, like fish. Nobody said anything except Gran who kept repeating: "Thank God, thank God," over and over. Sally-Anne knew she hadn't an ally among them, this time they were all on the other side.

Mum came a little way forward, holding her hands out as if she was acting in a play. She stopped when Dad asked "Where have you been?"

"There and back to see how far it was," she said cheekily, making a face.

Dad said: "I asked you where you had been."

"Ralph!" Mum said, and Dad said "Be quiet, Sal. We want to know where they have been."

"In the park, of course."

"The park!" Mum said, and snapped at Gran. "You see! I told you they were in the park all the time." Gran said "I can't run; you know I can't run."

"Your hair!" Mum said. "What happened?"

She put her hand up and found her hair was all pulled about and spiky, threaded through with bits of twigs.

"And your face!"

Her face was wet. She licked and it tasted salty, and when she rubbed her fingers across there was blood on them.

Dad said "You must tell your Mother and me how you got in that state."

She began to laugh, not because it was funny but because it was all so unreal. She couldn't stop, though laughing hurt. She hooted at their solemn faces. Now Boy was laughing, blowing out wet pink bubbles of gum until they exploded, making gloriously vulgar noises. They laughed and laughed.

"Stop that!" Dad was shaking her shoulders. "What happened? I want to know."

Boy stopped laughing and went over to Cousin Lionel and began to cry again, boo-hooing noisily. Cousin Lionel patted his hand and said: "It's all right son," over and over again. "There there, it's all right, it's all right," until Boy was quiet, turning off the tears like a tap, the way little kids do.

"Now tell us what happened."

She said "We ran after Punch, like Cousin Lionel said. I knew we hadn't a hope but he said run and so we ran. We ran and ran. We saw the ducks in the lake and he threw stones into the ice and jumped up and down on it until it cracked. When Gran and Cousin Lionel came to look for us we hid in the bushes and watched them going past. They were quite close. We heard what they were saying. If they'd looked properly they would have seen us. After they'd gone back we danced on the bandstand, only he can't dance. Then the bell rang and he wouldn't come and we nearly got shut in and the man shouted at us as we came out. I bought bubble-gum to stop him crying on the way home."

"Is that all?"

She could never remember disliking him so much before. "Except that we didn't want to go out, Gran and I. You and Mum sent us out so that you could be by yourselves."

"I asked if that was all."

"I know what you're thinking," she said, "you've got a one-track mind. But he's only a baby, really." She watched Dad's face as she said this, then wriggled free of him and ran full tilt for Mum.

Later, much later, bathed and brushed and comfortable, full of warm milk and aspirin, lying staring at the ceiling, redeemed and happy and home, hazily enjoying the aftermath of drama, she realised that something unusual was going on in the house. Doors opened and shut, voices were half heard on the telephone, there were cautious footsteps on the stairs. A car arrived and drove away again. The hall door closed. They came upstairs.

Mum said: "I'll move them tonight, Ralph," and her feet went backwards and forwards on the landing; the door of the spare room wardrobe creaked.

So Gran had gone and it was over. She tried to stay awake so that she could feel sorry for Gran, sorry and kind and safe, but it was no use; she never even heard Dad when he came in, or a single stroke of the clock.

CHAPTER EIGHT

"There! She's gone into the bathroom," Sheena said, easing her breast out of the baby's mouth. The baby hung on as long as possible, and when it let go the extended nipple sprang back like elastic. She heaved it up and propped it against her shoulder. "I told you—there's the water running. I hope she doesn't stay for hours and hours. Do you think she'll touch Philippa's ducks? She arranged them in a procession last night for you to see when you came in, only you were late and I forgot to tell you. Did you see them?"

"No," he said. "Sorry. I was tired."

"I wish you'd noticed, she spent hours," she worried. "Come on now, nice windies."

She smote the baby's back and it belched and dribbled. The thin blue milk still spurted from the wet cherry where the baby had been dislodged and ran down her breast. She put him back again. "Sam, yesterday I caught Martin fiddling with the key in the bathroom door. He wanted to know why we have a key now. I said because of Gran but of course he didn't understand."

"You can't really expect your mother to wash in the family circle."

"No, I suppose not." She pushed her fingers through her hair. "So long as it doesn't give him ideas, that's all. He thought it funny that anyone liked to be locked up in the bathroom."

"I hope he still thinks it's funny when he locks himself in."

"Oh dear, perhaps I should have tried to explain." She filed this idea away for future consideration, tightening her mouth over it. He wanted to take the baby away and pull her back on the pillow and kiss some softness into her.

"I suppose at Ralph and Sal's she had a bathroom all to herself."

"Wall-to-wall carpets and all mod. cons.," Sam said, "well, she hasn't got that here."

"How anyone can keep a carpet clean in a bathroom," Sheena said, "I mean—clean! I wonder what did happen at Sal's. She hasn't said a word, but something must have happened." The baby came off and gulped. "Oh dear, yesterday I ate onions, I hope it hasn't upset him. It was her, she wanted to help so I asked her to make the stew and she put onions in; you'd have thought she might have known."

"You could have told her."

"She'd done it. Of course I shouldn't have eaten any but I'm so famished all the time. And if he has pains now it's my fault."

"I don't know why it isn't a help to you, having your mother."

This one was too complex and Sheena missed it out, occupying herself with the baby. She mopped the oozing breast with her pyjama jacket and settled the baby against the other side. It snapped, missed, wailed, snapped again and made gluttonous contact.

He thought of Sheena's breasts, pearly and shy, emerging

from those honeymoon nightdresses. He wondered how much of what had happened to her was his fault and if it was always like this and whether she regretted it. Perhaps she did and this was her way of getting her own back on him. He thought of the three older children stretched flat under the bedclothes in their little beds in the other room, putting their faith in teddy bears until Mum and Dad were again available to them, and he was terrified.

"Anyway, what does she have to get up so early for? Wouldn't it be better if she had her breakfast in bed?"

"She's dusting the lounge before breakfast."

"Does it have to be dusted every day?"

"Her own lounge was."

"Women," he said. "Talk about the ancestral rites of savages. You know something, Sheena, you ought to write this down and promise to read it when Beth's married and you go to stay."

"Sam!" He was shocked and pleased at the ferocity with which she turned on him. She didn't often really see him nowadays, but she was seeing him this time.

"Do you think I'll really be like that?"

"Well-meaning and timid and bosomy with blue hair and plump ankles and incredible teeth."

She giggled; it was a long time since he'd succeeded in making Sheena giggle. "Mum isn't like that!"

"I'm talking about you," he mocked. He wondered if the baby would go to sleep straight off when it had gorged itself, and if his mother-in-law would stay in the bathroom long enough and whether there would be time, and if in any case

Sheena would want to. Mostly since the baby she didn't, and when she did he was sure that part of her was still totting up the money for the milkman or planning a meal or debating a new cure for Beth's nail-biting, as if it was a pity that the time should be spent solely on his necessities.

"Time's up," she said and unhooked the baby briskly. She kissed it and laid it in its cot and it bubbled a little and was quiet. She peeled off the top of her pyjamas—how many thousand customers of Marks and Spencers up and down the country were at this moment discarding an identical garment, he wondered, watching her—and flicked through the heap of clothes on her chair to find her vest. Turning with the top half of her body naked she said: "What do you suppose you'll be like in thirty years?" and stared for her answer.

"Bald and a paunch." Her indifference to her nakedness irritated him. Had she really no idea—? Probably not, nowadays Sheena made all the rules and nakedness was strictly neutral. "Come on," he urged. "Ah come here."

She turned her back at once. Of course she knew. "I can't, Sam."

"Don't sound so outraged, as if you were a Vestal Virgin or something. Why not?"

"You know there isn't time."

"She's still in the bathroom, you said she'd be there for hours. Ah, come on, Sheena."

"I can't, Sam. Really."

He got up and went to her. When he touched her she trembled and his heart bounded. "No, Sam. I told you I can't. Not now. Not with her here."

"For God's sake, Sheena, what difference is her being here supposed to make?"

"I can't explain. Please, Sam."

He cupped her shoulders with his palms. "Do you suppose she thinks we play ring-a-ring-a-roses? Is that what she did with your father?"

"There's no need to be coarse!"

She broke away from him and found her vest, whipped it over her head and pulled it down savagely. He sat on the edge of the bed cursing inwardly and fiddling with one of her garments. "Don't do that," she said, "you'll stretch the elastic." He threw it at her and she put it on.

"If your mother doesn't get a move on in the bathroom I'm going to be late, that's what. And there's a man coming down from head office."

She pulled a comb through her hair without looking in the mirror. "And this is Thursday. If breakfast is a rush then Martin won't have time to chew his egg properly."

"Why is Thursday a good day for chewing eggs?"

She turned with the comb in her hand and a look of horror. "Sam! You know. Thursday!"

"You look like something out of Greek Tragedy. What's wrong with Thursday?"

"It's Singing. You know he's frightened of Singing. If he gulps his egg he'll be sick like he was before. Don't you remember?"

"They're all sick all the time; none of it seems particularly memorable."

"Sam!"

"Oh all right, love. Sorry. But this man I was telling you about from head office—"

The baby bleated and she went and stood at the side of the cot making soothing noises while she pulled on her jersey. He wondered whether he could win her attention if he lay on his back screeching or pulled rude faces.

"Just how much longer do you suppose your mother's going to be in there?"

"Hush, Sam. The baby."

"This man," he persisted sulkily, "we don't want to look as if we were putting on a special show for him or anything; really it's just an informal visit."

"What did you say?"

He heard his mother-in-law vacating the bathroom.

"Nothing. It doesn't matter."

She zipped up her slacks. "I thought perhaps it did."

Later, across the wrecked breakfast table (the older children upstairs loudly competing for the lavatory, Philippa off to rearrange the procession of ducks which Gran had disturbed, Sheena having mopped up the mess of Martin's vomited egg now busy with the baby again) he confronted his mother-in-law. She looked tired and small, stroking butter across a piece of toast but making no attempt to eat it.

"It wasn't like this at Ralph and Sal's," he suggested, wondering what it had been like, but she didn't rise. "This sort of domestic hooly is very funny when you see it on strip cartoons, and on picture postcards and Comedy Hour on the telly it's a perfect scream."

"You get the saccharin version in the glossy magazines,"

she said. The toast had broken and her fingers were greasy. She looked for the napkin that wasn't there and used her handkerchief. "It's really very clever how the glossies manage to sanctify it, but half the letters are from husbands asking Aunt Edna how to steer overworked wives back to romance and what to do with wives who have gone frigid through sheer exhaustion. Sheena used to giggle herself silly over them when she was a girl."

"What does Aunt Edna advise?"

"Mostly 'Bring her home a bunch of flowers and she falls panting into your arms again.'"

"She hasn't the time," he said, staring with interest at the stranger who was Sheena's mother. "Anyway, what a load of tripe. And we don't have that sort of cash in this house. What are you going to do today?"

"I am wheeling out the baby."

Curiously he asked "You never call him Harry, do you? I've noticed."

"Not yet."

He wondered whether, thirty years on, any female infant labelled with Sheena's name would make any difference to him if he had lost Sheena. He felt very frightened.

"It was very thoughtful and kind of you and Sheena to decide to give the baby that name," his mother-in-law said, "and I do appreciate it. When Sheena was a little girl she gave her dolls all the names she said she was going to give her children, but I'm glad she didn't go through with it, some of them were frightful.'

"Did she have a lot of dolls?"

"Dozens. Oh dear, she hasn't even touched her tea."

"Would it be any good taking it up?"

"What do you think?"

He decided against it. He rose to go, and on an impulse told her about the man who was coming down from head office. "Of course we won't be putting on any special sort of a show for him; just a casual visit, really."

She nodded and said: "You couldn't ever make Sheena do anything unless she wanted to. Liz was different, she had a conscience, poor child. But Sheena—pretty as a picture and obstinate as a mule."

He made his excuses and bolted. You couldn't win. He called goodbye up the stairs, making a last minute bid for Sheena's blessing.

She came out onto the landing and called: "What is it, Sam?" He knew that pointedly patient voice.

"Nothing," he said bleakly. "I'm just off."

Later Julia wheeled the pram through the park. The morning was calm and filled with thin February sunshine. Philippa had stayed at home with her mother. She had been fretful and naughty. Sheena thought the trouble was connected with the ducks' procession in the bathroom, it was a pity Gran hadn't understood their significance and had tidied them. So Julia had her grandson to herself, but she was disturbed rather than elated by the self-satisfied infant on its pillow.

"Yes, 'Harry'. Wasn't it sweet of them?" she had told her friends, wondering what the bestowing of the name should have done to her and glad in secret that it did nothing at all. They had been eager for her to be touched by the choice as if this Harry's birth did something to balance Harold's death.

There were few people in the park. Rooks squabbled in the upper reaches of the elms, and small birds fussed through the dry leaves at the base of the trees, dislodging them from frost-packed heaps. Snowdrops were fully open and the strong blades of the daffodils had just broken their way into the air. The buds on the ash trees were intensely black.

She sat down for a while on a bench and reread the letter she had had that morning from Ralph. It amused, exasperated and touched her. He had written the letter with care. He hoped she had not allowed herself to be distressed by what had happened, it was only natural and to be expected that such a situation might arise. Young people were always unpredictable, were they not, his mother with her experience would recognise that. They both perfectly understood her motive in leaving and hoped she had not misinterpreted theirs in not insisting that she should stay. Knowing her he felt sure that she had not. Sal and Sally-Anne sent their love. With anxious affection he succeeded in rationalising the events of her visit. "Human nature being what it is" he wrote. It was, after what had happened, a good letter, and she was grateful for it.

The child's quick breathing ruffled the fluff of the blanket. The successor to Harold's breath. An old gentleman came by, smiled and peered at the complacent child. He lifted his hat. "Spring in the air," he said. Spring in the air and earth turning urgently towards warmth again, and Harold taking no part in it, Harold cancelled, overlooked. Birds sang and children shouted. She wheeled the pram home, the infant woke and smiled and waved his fists in a passion of living.

Lunch was ready. Sheena apologised defiantly for the slice of corned beef and the dismal salad. "I'm sorry." She catalogued the morning's catastrophes.

"I wish you'd let me do some more of the cooking for you, dear."

Sheena was too busy fielding trickles of broth from Philippa's chin and putting them back in her mouth to answer. Later she nursed the baby who was whimpering and ate her salad, single-handed.

Halfway through the meal—tinned creamed rice and jam coming up—Beth arrived unexpectedly bringing Martin home from school. "He's been sick again," she reported. "They said he ought to come. I'm missing French to bring him. French is my favourite."

Martin looked cheerful and said he was hungry.

"I thought you'd been sick."

"I know."

At the word "sick" Philippa blew out her broth descriptively. Some of it spattered the baby.

Julia said: "Let me take him from you."

"It's all right." With magnificent control Sheena asked Beth if she would be in time to have school dinner when she got back. Beth didn't know. Probably not. It was jelly cream —her favourite.

"I'd better have something here in case," she said.

Sheena said they'd almost finished. Beth said she supposed she could have bread, couldn't she, or would she just starve?

"I'm hungry," Martin said.

"I didn't finish my meat," Julia suggested. "Help me to clear the plate."

"He doesn't like corned beef, Mum," Sheena said.

Martin ate his grandmother's corned beef with relish, looking sideways at his mother to see what effect he was producing. Beth sighed noisily and attacked the loaf with a martyr's vigour, the knife slipped and her finger spurted red.

Martin said: "Look what she's done! Silly ass!"

Beth waved her finger in dismay and blood dripped into the dish of creamed rice.

Martin laughed loudly with his mouth full of corned beef. Suddenly Sheena got up and gave the baby to her mother and went round the table and pulled Martin off his chair and hit him, and stopped and looked at him and hit him again.

In the long shocked silence that followed, Beth wound her hankie round her finger and went back to school, munching, the baby fell asleep and Julia put him into his carrycot, Philippa stopped wailing and plodded upstairs again, grumbling about her Quacky Ducks. Martin polished off the corned beef and announced that he was going into the garden to play.

Julia said: "All right. Go on."

Sheena had said nothing except "Oh God, Oh God, Oh God!" Her voice was flat, appalled, tired out. She was sitting at the table with her forearms lying across it and her head slumped. At last she sat up and challenged her mother. "What have I done? What have I done?"

"You slapped him," Julia said calmly, "he was extremely

naughty and tiresome and he deserved it. It was much the best thing to do."

"Mother!" Sheena was scandalised.

"Of course if you want to make high drama out of it you can." Julia began to tidy up the shambles of the meal. Sheena sat and watched but didn't stir.

"I've never hit any of them. Never. I've always explained. This could have terrible effects on him. Nothing like this has ever happened to him before."

Julia looked into the garden and saw the swing travelling through the air and Martin crouched on it, joyfully forcing it higher and higher.

"All kinds of things are going to happen to him," she said briskly, "you'd better get used to the idea."

"What sort of things?"

My poor tired frightened little girl. Julia concentrated on getting rid of the blood-streaked rice pudding; she stirred it with her finger as she turned the tap on to wash it down the sink. The swinging boy shot in and out of the sunlight.

"People will be cruel to him for no reason that he can understand. And friends will cheat him, and he'll discover that the Baddies are much more likely to win than lose. And when he goes away from home he may be ill or lonely or homesick and without comfort. People he cares for will die. He'll find out what sex does to him and what success and disappointment are like and how much he can ask God for. This is all going to happen. And there may be a nuclear war."

"I don't think I can bear it."

The last of the mess was washed away. "Don't be silly, you

138

have to," Julia said. She made tea and poured a cup and set it at Sheena's elbow. "Drink up. I'm going out this afternoon."

She poured a cup for herself and drank it, and before she left the kitchen she saw that Sheena had lifted her cup and was dredging through the biscuit tin.

Her knees were unsteady as she went upstairs. She wanted at every step to turn back full of reassurance and false comforts. Sheena would have been ready for them all.

Ralph, of course, is right, the domestic pattern repeats over and over again, we can't escape it. My own performance wasn't any improvement on Sheena's. I tell myself that I was magnificent, but I wasn't. I was just as harassed and over anxious and absurd, and I wonder how my poor Harold, with his love for smooth living, ever put up with me during those long years when bed-wetting and nightmares and thumb-sucking were more important than anything he had to offer me. Even his leaves were full of them. Air raids upset me less than temperatures and temper and constipation and milk that boiled over on the stove. I wonder if Sheena has any clear memory of me as I was then, or if I was just a symbol of security that had no right to feelings or aspirations of its own, and whether in the end it had any value for her or for any of them. We invent the importance of what we are doing be-cause it is the only way we could get through it. We make mountains out of molehills because we need to have some sort of scenery. I can't tell her that; in any case she wouldn't believe me.

Her resolution took her to the top of the stairs. She was glad she hadn't gone back though she recognised with appalled delight that after so much careful self-discipline she had committed the unforgiveable sin of Knowing Best.

Philippa was in the bathroom, chattily marshalling her ducks. She was in a benevolent mood and held their plastic beaks up to be kissed. "Nice Gran," she said, growing maudlin with love, and rubbing against Julia's knees, "quacky ducks love nice Gran." Julia picked her up, a solid damp little person, they exchanged treasonable affection. "Sing," Philippa commanded. Julia sat on the edge of the bath and sang. The ducks sang through their plastic beaks. Philippa sang. The sun shone through the squares of coloured glass at the corners of the bathroom windows, making bright lozenge shapes on the sides of the bath. Philippa grew more solid and fell asleep. Her lids lay so lightly on her cheeks that the whites of her eyes still glinted through her lashes. Julia carried her to her cot, unwound her arms from her own neck and arranged a reception committee of ducks on the pillow, to greet her when she woke. There was no sound anywhere in the house when she let herself out of the hall door twenty minutes later.

Johnnie was in his book shop. She stood watching him through the glass door, this is how he looks to other people. He was talking to a customer, the girl with pale smooth hair. He looked up and saw his mother. She hoped it was going to be all right, inwardly rebellious that she needed to apologise about coming unannounced into his public world. Then he said something to the girl and smiled a welcome at Julia and she went in.

When they were alone Julia said "What a nice girl, who is she?"

"Just a nice girl." He grinned and kissed her. "I was afraid you would smell of baby powder but you don't."

He brought her into the cupboard that he called his office and found a chair for her. He made a charming host. She sat pulling her gloves off slowly, finger by finger, wishing it could always be like this. She had come to the right place, she hoped the party would go on long enough.

"I suppose it's frightful at Sheena's," he said.

She frowned reproof and said "I don't see why it should be."

"Always so loyal," he teased, "I don't know how you do it."

"Sam and Sheena are very happy, Johnnie."

"When she has time," he said.

He filled a kettle and lit the gas under it, and then went to the shop next door and came back with a paper bag full of cream cakes. The kettle boiled and he made tea, concentrating heavily on the mathematics of cups and spoonsful and boiling water. "Lovely," she said, watching him, "just what I need."

He asked when she was coming back to the house. She took a perverse pleasure is not enquiring whether he was missing her.

"I suppose you are coming back, aren't you?"

"I suppose so, some time. They say it's better for me not to be by myself too much."

"Who says?"

"The girls."

He didn't say: "You wouldn't be by yourself, I'd be there." Instead he asked seriously: "And is it better for you?"

She was too moved and happy to answer. Since Harold died her relations with the children had been thrown out of balance, she was half of a pair, a relict, an object for concern, incomplete. But this could be the beginning of something new; light and easy and intimate. Perhaps at last he would allow her to stop being his mother.

Johnnie said: "I don't suppose it's good for anybody to live too much by themselves."

"Johnnie, that's a curious sentiment, coming from you."

"I'm different," he shrugged.

"I don't see why."

"Are you scheming to tie me up with some Nice Girl? Can you imagine me being any good at it?"

"Of course I can."

"It wouldn't be any use."

"Why not?"

He didn't answer right away. Then he said: "Because it terrifies me, didn't you know? I thought that was the kind of thing you would have known about me, you missed a trick there, didn't you? I don't mean I'm frightened of sex—I believe in going in for sex in a big way and suffering anguish in between my loves. But Heaven preserve me from domesticity and a Nice Girl."

"But, Johnnie," she floundered, and stopped. It was no use, the teaparty was spoiled, he had seen that she was unwillingly embarrassed, whoever said "sex" first turned on the red light.

"Idylls may be up your street but they aren't up mine, you must know that," he said roughly, " 'Till Death Us Do Part'." He hesitated and asked "Does it, by the way?"

"No. At least I don't think so."

"That's something to be thankful for, you don't have to suffer the anguish."

"Johnnie please—"

He insisted: "I only said you must be very glad it doesn't part."

Angrily she said: "I'm not sure if I am. It isn't as easy as all that."

"But of course you are, you must be!" He sounded outraged. Poor Johnnie. So the idyll was part of his pattern too, he didn't want it destroyed. In some obscure way it was still valuable to him. "You must be glad," he persisted.

She put down her cup and gathered her gloves. "I have the rest of my life, remember that," she said briskly, and went back to Sheena's.

There was calm and a feeling of exhausted peace in the house. She found Sheena and the family at the tea-table. Sam had not yet come home.

"Gran's back!"

They were glad to see her, they made her welcome. The meal continued. There was no argument or bickering, a lot of silly jokes went amiably round the table. No one showed off. There were no spilled mugs. Everyone's egg was just right. Beth had brought comics home from school, she gave some of them to Martin. He had been on the swing all afternoon, had worked himself a fine appetite. Philippa was benignly funny with her rusks. The baby lay and smiled like a seraph on his mother's knee. Sheena's face was pale but relaxed, she presided over them wearily but with love. And they loved each other devotedly over the bread and jam and boiled eggs, they stretched their happiness out to include Julia. She remembered times like this when her family had seemed suddenly to bloom into a sublime and golden whole. The plates had been almost cleared when they heard Sam's step in the hall.

"Daddy's back!" they cried, "Daddy!"

The door opened. Sam stood there almost obscured by the great bunch of sugar pink carnations. Behind them his eyes and teeth gleamed nervously.

"Look! Mummy look! See what Daddy's brought!" Sheena had not yet spoken.

Oh you great silly ass, you well intentioned blunderer, how obvious and mistaken can you get? Don't you remember she despises carnations, she wouldn't let you wear one in your buttonhole at the wedding. It's always carnations we told her but no, not for Sheena, it was rosebuds all round. Pink, too. Sweet pink. What an absurd posy, what a conventional, ridiculous gesture. Can't you see that she is already converting the flowers into meals and shoe leather and school dinner tickets?

Sheena stood up and passed the baby to her mother. She held on to the edge of the table for what seemed a very long time. Then she said "Sam! Sam!" The children rose in a mass and fought their way towards the door. Sam held the flowers above his head at arm's length. Sheena got there first.

Two hours later Julia knocked at Johnnie's flat and asked if he could give her milk for her breakfast. He supposed he could. He looked sulky and not altogether pleased to see her. She had tried Liz first, she explained, but Liz wasn't upstairs.

"She's out praising the Lord," Johnnie said, "he comes back with her for supper now. What are you doing here anyhow? I thought you were safely tucked up with Sam and Sheena."

"I decided suddenly I wanted to come home."

"What did you say to Sheena?"

"That you told me this afternoon the painters were coming in the morning to paint the bathroom."

"Are they?"

"I don't think so." She smiled, trying to involve him in the conspiracy but there wasn't a glimmer. She'd had her chance this afternoon, he was still a little raw from that.

"Why the hurry, anyhow?"

This she couldn't explain. Envy for their happiness, the laughter, the children with carnations in their hair packed off to bed one by one, clowning all the way, Sam and Sheena restless and polite with love like a flame between them. So she had run away. She hoped for a welcome. There wasn't going to be any.

With an oppressive air of duty Johnnie came to carry her case upstairs for her.

"No letters," she said shuffling through the buff envelopes and circulars. "Only bills. And I don't know what's happened to Madge these days. Not a word from her all the time I was at Ralph's and Sheena's."

"I expect she's busy."

"Madge! Madge is never too busy to come here, you know that."

"She could have troubles of her own," he suggested.

Something in his voice held her. "Troubles? What sort of troubles?"

"Anguish for instance," he said, and put down her case.

CHAPTER NINE

"I don't feel anything," she said, "not anything at all. It isn't that I'm trying not to. I want to feel something, even though Harold mightn't have wished me to. But I just go on in an empty muddled kind of way, getting impatient because I'm always waiting for some piercing grief that doesn't come. I mean I don't suppose this is all there is to it, it couldn't be, could it? I thought at the beginning it was shock but it's four months now."

The daffodils in the metal container were caught and toppled by a gust of wind. She bent to straighten them, and then stood erect, drying her fingers on the handkerchief she had expected to need for her eyes.

Mildred said "It's perishing up here. You should have had a scarf. You'll catch a chill."

"Are you cold?"

"No, no. I'm quite all right. I was only worrying about you."

Mildred didn't look all right; there was an air of doom about her, her face was patchy and her eyes anticipated distress. Probably the unbecoming hat was a gesture in deference to the solemnity of the cemetery, which was sweet of her but mistaken. Her mouth was drawn in and small, she must be cold. She ought to do something about her teeth, one could always spot National Health; one wondered if perhaps Wilfred was a little mean about that kind of thing and how thoughts like these could enter one's mind a few yards from the spot where one's body, empty of all thought, would eventually lie.

"It was good of you to come with me, Mildred."

"Oh I wanted to," Mildred panted—emotion perhaps, or the effort at climbing the hill—"I was so pleased you'd asked me. I said to the girls at breakfast 'Julia wants me to go with her to take flowers.' I thought you'd have asked Madge." Under her deep brim Mildred yearned. The wind snatched at the hat and she caught it just in time.

Julia didn't tell her that she had in fact asked Madge, but Madge couldn't make it. "Someone else has been here." She stooped to lift a bunch of small withered flowers and set them aside. "I think these have been violets."

"One of the children, I suppose."

"They didn't mention it. It's peculiar, we mourn him privately, they never talk."

"Children are like that."

"But they keep a watchful eye to see that I'm behaving properly."

"What do they call properly? No, don't tell me dear, I don't think I ought to let you talk like this."

"Why not?" There is something about gravestones that tempts confidences even in the teeth of a searing March wind. "They would like me to be discreetly desolate, I think."

The wind carried her voice away. "What was that you said?" Mildred screeched.

"Discreetly desolate!"

148

"And—are you?" The wind couldn't disguise the fascinated curiosity in Mildred's voice. "Desolate, I mean."

"That's what I'm telling you. I don't feel anything very much. Even now, when I'm standing here—wouldn't you think that standing here—"

"Now you're getting morbid and you mustn't," Mildred fussed, "I promised Cora I wouldn't let you get morbid."

"I don't see what it's got to do with Cora. You shouldn't have said you were coming."

"Even if I hadn't they'd have found out," Mildred cried peevishly. "Careful, Julia, the wind's going to knock the daffodils over again, you'll have to jam the vase some way. They seem to think they have a right to know everything about me. I wonder sometimes if it's a revenge for the time when they were little girls, unconscious revenge, of course. Do you remember how sweet they were, Julia, like glass, so bright and fragile and transparent—I knew everything about them, even what they were thinking, as if they lived inside my hands." Mildred collected the tails of hair which had escaped from her hat and pushed them back, embarrassed by the success of this verbal extravagance.

Julia hunted through her bag and found a nail-file and used it to scrape the soil from below the vase, to give it a more stable base. "Children have such odd ideas. The other day Johnnie insisted that my married life had been one long idyll."

"How peculiar of him. I always loathed Tennyson, anyway."

"You what?"

149

"Tennyson—I loathed him. Have you nearly finished?"

"In a minute. I think that was what Johnnie wanted to believe. Children are very cunning that way. He was hoping I'd agree with him."

"I thought idylls were out, anyway."

"For him and his generation, maybe, but he'd have been more comfortable if he thought he was a child of that kind of love. I don't think one really cares for the idea of violent sex between one's parents, do you? Passion seems—unbecoming. I never imagined mine as having any kind of sex life one way or another, they were never sufficiently separate from each other to need it, or do you think I was deliberately pushing the idea out of my subconscious or whatever it is?"

"Come on, Julia; that vase is all right now."

"Johnnie says it was an idyll and Madge maintains that Harold and I were the victims of a great purple passion. Of course I told her—"

"Come on. There's a funeral arriving. We don't want to get tangled up in it."

"All right, I'm coming." In any case we can't carry on this conversation any longer at the tops of our voices. Julia stood up trying to find some way of removing the soil from her nail file before she put it back in her bag. All at once the problem seemed insurmountable. "He was a good man," she said, "oh dear, oh dear!"

"Come *on*!"

Mildred gripped her elbow firmly and steered her past the incoming trickle of mourners, and by the time they had reached the car her eyes were clear again.

"I'm sorry," she apologised, "I don't know what I'd do without you." Mildred's face flushed and softened. "Tea and buns at the Copper Kettle," she said.

Warm and dry and with the sense of mission accomplished they sat at a small table in the Copper Kettle. The rain beat on the window—cold rain drenching down on the daffodils, soaking the earth, the bones laid in the earth, one must not allow oneself to think of that, such thoughts are indecent, that is what Harold would have felt about them, so one is excused for pushing them out of the way and accepting the warm sweet tea. Julia relaxed, all images were blurred. Across the table Mildred, slightly out of focus, looked untypically noble.

Mildred chattered about the St. Matthew Passion which the Choral were rehearsing for Easter. It was going to be wonderful, Julia must be sure to come. One felt positively eternal, not a doubt left anywhere. (An uneasy moment here, a quick offer of buttered crumpets, balance restored.) Of course the Passion wasn't nearly so helpful as the Messiah, there was this ghastly guilt all the time. Did one really need to feel guilty? Guilt was difficult. The girls, Mildred said, made her feel guilty most of the time. The waitress came up with cakes on the trolley, and waited with tongs poised. "Cora is dieting, I am terrified to eat at home, she watches every mouthful I take and suffers tortures, poor girl," Mildred said, and asked the waitress to give her a cream slice and an éclair.

Julia said: "Those flowers on the grave, the little faded bunch that I thought were violets. They must have come from Madge."

151

Closing on the first mouthful Mildred said: "I wondered about that. She grows violets, doesn't she?"

"Then why did you say it was one of the children?"

Mildred's tongue tidied up neatly, cream and lipstick. "It could have been one of the children," she said.

"No. Those were the ceremonial first fruits. Madge was dotty about Harold. Surely you knew that?"

Below her brim Mildred's eyes were guarded but eager. She leaned a little closer. "I wasn't sure if you knew."

"My dear, of course. Even before I met Madge I could tell just by the way he talked. Affectionate and a little scornful."

"Could you really?"

"His sweet childhood's playmate. They all have them. It's rather touching really. I expect Wilfred's the same, isn't he?"

"My dear, need you ask, the scene is littered with them. From Land's End to John O'Groats Wilfred played, every game in the book."

"Poor Millie, how wretched for you."

"They keep turning up in between his present fancies, quite haggish some of them." Mildred sucked her fingers. They asked the waitress to bring more hot water.

"I don't think Madge ever really came out of the Lower Sixth," Julia said. "What was she like at school?"

"Scruffy and didn't wash her neck, always terribly intense about everything."

Julia leaned back feeling smoothed and happy. "I wonder what happened to tomboys—like Art Nouveau or something, they were so fashionable and then they simply disappeared.

Except old Madge. He used to call her 'Old Madge'. Women who suffer from that kind of hero-worship ought to be compelled to go to bed with their heroes, don't you think?"

"Julia!" Poor dear Mildred, scandalised, fascinated, inflamed with tea.

"Red hot passion between ice cold sheets—you know the sort of thing."

But Mildred was really disconcerted, she ought to think of going, the girls would wonder why she was so late, Cora would think something had happened to her coming back in the middle of the rush hour, supper mightn't be on time, this was Cora's night for her Madrigal Group.

"Julia! My dear! What is the matter? Was it something I said?"

"It's all right. No really—only being stupid." But without any warning Julia was weeping gently into the crumbs of her cream cake.

"Quite all right in a minute."

"But what was it?"

"It's like this all the time," she explained, mopping up and feeling terrible, "little things when you don't expect them. Nothing immense. Just little things."

"What little thing was it?"

"Madrigals. Harold used to go to those Madrigal evenings. I suddenly thought of him. I'm not being sentimental or anything like that, Millie, and I don't like Madrigals particularly; he used to take it all so seriously and looked so silly, such a large man being so very careful over such a small note—"

"My dear, I'm sorry. I simply had no idea."

"How could you? I'm all right now."

"Sure?"

"Quite sure."

The incident had brought them closer. Beneath the table their knees offered warmth to each other's knees. They drained their cups in silence, avoiding each other's eyes.

"I suppose we ought to go now."

"I suppose so."

"You said Cora was going out."

"Yes, I know. You're staying with Ralph, aren't you? That's nice."

"I was."

"Not now?"

"No. I was with Sheena too for a while."

"Oh?" Mildred's restraint was heroic.

"But I'm back at my own house again."

"I see."

Julia lowered her voice. "Mildred, tell me, did you have children because you wanted to perpetuate yourself?"

Mildred looked startled. "Perpetuate myself? Good gracious no, such a thing never crossed my mind." Other pleasanter things that might have crossed her mind softened her face.

"You mean you weren't planting stakes in the future, or whatever it is?"

"I certainly was not. Were you?"

"No. When I'm old and dying the idea may console me, at the moment it leaves me cold."

"Julia! How can you? You're always so wonderful with your children."

154

"I'll tell you something. I got away from Ralph's and I got away from Sheena's, and I'm not going back."

"Do you mean that, Julia?"

"Certainly."

"Oh Julia! What will you do?"

"I think I will go on a tour of Old Ladies' Homes and book myself in for a nice room wherever I think best. Then, when I need to be washed and fed that's where I'll go."

"I do so admire you, you're wonderful. That is the best thing, of course."

"We might move in together, Mildred. It's an idea."

"It would be simply marvellous but the girls would never think of it. And there's Wilfred, of course. But I'll come and help you look."

"The girls, the girls! Can't you ever get away from them?"

Something like terror crept in at the back of Mildred's moist eyes. "I can't. I don't think I want to."

"The way they bully you—"

"I know, I know."

"Then why?"

Mildred stroked her gloves and said: "Can't you see I have to be some use to somebody. Sometimes I'm ashamed, the way I scheme so that they'll allow me to be involved in their lives—little things, like fetching their clothes from the cleaners or taking telephone messages. I'd crawl, Julia, just for the crumbs. If I don't have this everything just stops."

"What sort of pleasure do you get out of it?"

"Like when I felt them kindle, Julia. It's like that."

"Or at the breast," Julia said.

"I wouldn't know about that, I was dry as a bone, every time." Her ineffectual features pled for Julia's sympathy. "You're still pretty, Julia, and amusing; you can dress up and go about and have smart friends and parties. I'm not like that. If it wasn't for Wilfred and the children I can't think of any reason why I shouldn't just sit with my hands folded until I die quietly—"

"That's absurd."

"And they're very good to me, really. I get these tiresome heads, it must be a nuisance for them. And Wilfred can't really help being the way he is, I suppose it's my fault he needs to run after girls. They say men do. I think secretly he's terrified that some day he'll—well, if he does it will be my fault. You see it in the paper sometimes, quite respectable men. I knew from the beginning of course that he was marrying me as—a kind of refuge—"

"What were you marrying him for?"

"I was so grateful. And then of course I'd have done anything to get away from Mamma—oh dear, oh dear!" The chatter and tinkle of the tea-shop seemed to be suspended so that her words fell into a pool of silence. She flushed scarlet and sat in confusion, appalled, staring at Julia. "What have I said?"

Suddenly in Mildred's foolishness Julia saw a kind of salvation, it was as if lights had just gone on.

Mildred was tearing her paper napkin into very small shreds and scattering them on her plate. "If there was anyone who needed me—anyone at all."

"There is."

156

Mildred looked up, not understanding fully but already silly with hope. "Who?"

"I need you. I'm planning a holiday and I wanted to ask if you would come with me."

Mildred's mouth thickened. She gathered the scraps of paper and tightened her fingers on them, reducing them to a hard pellet. She allowed this to drop on her plate. "You weren't. You were going on a tour of Old Ladies' Homes."

"That was after I came back."

"Really?"

"Really."

"You're only saying that because you're kind. And I couldn't anyway. And you're upsetting me by asking."

"You really are a chinless mule, Millie. I don't wonder you drive Cora and the girls scatty."

"Don't scold. I do, I know I do!" she moaned, sagging.

"We drive them scatty, they drive us scatty, much more sensible if we both admit it; and it's worse, you know, when there are grandchildren."

"Is it? I thought it would be better."

"Much worse," Julia promised. "So complicated, minds within minds, a wilderness of toes to tread on. For example what would you say when your grand-daughter told you that after her pet kitten died her other Grannie said it had gone to play in Jesus' garden, and did you think this was really true?"

"What *did* you say?"

Julia chuckled. "Told her to ask her mother," she said, wishing she could have witnessed Sal's reaction.

157

"I should never have been able to think of anything so subtle as that. Oh dear."

"So cheer up, Millie, and come on this holiday with me. It would be good for me to have a holiday, but not good to go on my own. You could tell Cora and the girls that. You could say I'd asked you specially to go with me, to tide me over a bad time."

"Oh Julia." Beneath their powder Mildred's cheeks burned. "We couldn't—could we?"

"We could. If you'd like to."

"It would be bliss," Mildred breathed.

This was questionable, but it was too late now to retract, the seed of rebellion was sown and bliss sometimes came unexpectedly. I shall become some curious eccentric if I live alone, indulging myself in absurd ways to prove that I exist; I shall dwindle to nothing if I live with the children. Mildred will provide me with the landscape that I need—we both need a landscape. I'll try Mildred—if she'll come.

"I'll come."

"Oh Millie. I hoped you would."

"Of course you shouldn't go alone, it would be most unwise, I wouldn't dream of it." Mildred was halfway there already. "I will send the girls postcards from all kinds of interesting places. Not once a week, you know, but just whenever I happen to think of it."

"Good for you."

"We might meet some quite amusing people, don't you think?"

"We will, of course we will."

Like conspirators they laid their plot. They would go straight to the travel agent before returning home, if they made haste he would still be there, he would promise them provisional bookings and they could collect brochures and leaflets, then they would have something positive with which to confront the children.

"I wonder what they'll say when I tell them," Mildred mused, but with curiosity rather than apprehension. "Where are we going, Julia?"

"I was thinking Switzerland might be rather nice. Would you like that?"

"I'd adore it. A couple of autumn crocuses, or was that Austria?" Mildred giggled. "Oh Julia!" Her eye gleamed, she said she would ring up Cora at her office right away. Cora hated being rung at the office. She would tell Cora that Julia had insisted she should go back to her house for supper—they had plans they wanted to discuss—"I won't say what plans, not yet"—and would Cora hunt about and find something for herself and the girls in the frig, there was sure to be something. "There isn't. I told them I'd bring fish. Oh dear, perhaps after all—"

"Mont Blanc and the Matterhorn," Julia prompted, "we can't weaken, not now!"

"Cowbells and eidelweiss," Mildred cried, " 'The shades of night were falling fast, Upidee Upidah, When through an Alpine village passed, Upideeidah! A youth who bore mid snow and ice, A banner with this strange device—' I used to get prizes for Modern Languages at school, did anyone ever tell you? I don't suppose anyone remembers."

They had finished supper (a slovenly affair in front of the fire with their shoes kicked off and maps and brochures and time-tables pushed around among the plates and the coffee cups and the bottle of wine Mildred had insisted on buying on the way home) and Mildred's hair had just come down for the second time from sheer pleasure when the bell rang.

"Oh dear—are you expecting anyone?"

"It's probably Cora," Julia teased.

Mildred made a grand gesture, knocking over the mustard. "Come right in, Cora!"

It wasn't Cora. It was Ralph, worried and righteous, and Sheena, untidy and tearful. Julia's heart sank. She wasn't ready for them yet, and a great deal more work needed to be done on Mildred.

"Can we come in?"

"Of course, dears. What a lovely surprise."

Ralph's face mutely contradicted her. He didn't say anything until the door had closed. His opening words were prepared. "I called round at Sheena's to see how you were and to bring you some magazines from Sal and I found you weren't there."

"I came home a few days ago."

"Sheena told me. She said you said you were having painters in to do the bathroom." How like Harold you are when you say that.

"I see. So you did a little research and found I wasn't."

"Yes." She saw the painful flicker of impatience on his face and felt humble and sorry, wanting to put her hands up to comfort him, but this is a thing one can't do any longer, there are only words and one doesn't know the language.

"I'm sorry, Ralph. I thought I was better at home. You have all been very kind—"

Sheena said "I'm sure we did everything we could."

"You did, dear, you did!"

"Sam and the children were quite upset when you went off like that."

"I'm sorry."

"If you'd just told us," Ralph said. "You must realise we're concerned about you."

"Yes, Ralph. Of course."

How staid and sweet and kind of them to be concerned. Their concern threatened her. She was rescued by the bell ringing for a second time. Ralph said "Who on earth—" He opened the door. This time it was Cora.

"Is Mother here?"

"Yes, dear. Do come in," Julia said.

Cora came in. The hall was becoming crowded.

"Where is Mother?"

"We were just finishing supper."

There was no choice but to lead the way to the drawing-room. Mildred with her feet up and hairpins in her mouth stared at them. She is going to spoil it, it will all be spoiled, there is no defence on earth against dutiful affection.

Mildred ran the last hairpin home and asked: "Is this a committee meeting or something?" She disentangled herself from the wreckage of the meal and stood up, feeling around with stockinged feet for her shoes. "What is it, Cora? Is anything the matter, dear?"

Cora blinked. "No of course not. It was just so odd, getting your message like that. I mean it wasn't like you. I wondered if anything was wrong—"

"Wrong? Why on earth should something be wrong?" Mildred leaned back against the mantelpiece.

"It was so odd."

"Of course there's nothing wrong, dear, how very sweet and silly of you to be fussed." How magnificently she did it, teasing, keeping it friendly and casual—"my daughter and I, just like two sisters" the kind of thing one always imagined oneself doing and that never came off. "You found yourselves some supper, I hope?"

"Yes." Cora was so riveted by her mother's behaviour that the sardines and pallid potatoes faded from her mind.

"Good for you. Actually I was just coming along. Julia and I have had such fun planning our little holiday."

"Holiday?"

"It's so very sweet of her to ask me to go with her."

"Lovely that she can come," Julia said, "and with her languages it will make things twice as easy for me. I'm absolutely hopeless."

"Languages?"

"My Italian's hopelessly rusty, I'm afraid."

"Ah, but your French and German!"

Cora swallowed and said: "Where are you going?"

Her mother gathered travel leaflets from the sofa as if she

162

were picking a bunch of flowers. "Well, we've a lot of planning to do yet, and we don't want to be too tied down. Sils Maria, I think—a little place outside St. Moritz, you wouldn't know it—and we must find out if Cousin Roger is at Davos, Julia, get him to invite us somewhere amusing for lunch." She was overplaying madly, but no one seemed to have noticed. They were taking it more calmly than Julia had anticipated—more than this, when they recoiled from the first shock they said what a splendid idea, how kind of Julia, how lovely it would be at this time of year. Their eyes were guarded, their voices brittle. They're relieved, Julia realised, and stifled the idea that she'd have preferred it if they hadn't been quite so ready to let her go. Ralph was already rationalising the escapade at the back of his mind, planning what he would say to Sal.

Mildred told Cora to hurry off now like a good girl or she would be late for her Madrigals, and Cora went off meekly, still slightly shocked. Ralph and Sheena faded. Julia gave Mildred black coffee to steady her up. Before she went Mildred said: "Are we a couple of troublesome and malicious old ladies, Julia?"

"I don't think so."

"I don't much mind, anyway," Mildred said. "Once they'd got used to the idea they were glad, didn't you notice?"

"I wondered if you did."

They avoided each other's eyes and kissed, and Mildred went home.

Julia was tidying the mess of the meal when Liz knocked and came in. She wanted some coffee, had Julia any?

"Take it, take it, it's over there." Thank God for one child who doesn't care what I do on my side of the fence provided I stay there. "Can't you find it—try the top shelf."

"I've got it, thanks," Liz said, and didn't move.

"Having friends in?"

"A friend. William, his name is. You know. He was here the other day."

"Is that all you want?"

"Just the coffee."

More than coffee, my girl. There is something you want to tell me about and I don't want to be told, not this evening. I am tired and confused and your father is lying under a precariously perched vase of daffodils and all I want is to get into bed and fall asleep before the idea of Mildred skipping about the Alps like a chamois begins to trouble my imagination. Mildred and I have won a formidable battle; whatever it is you have come to tell me I don't want to hear it now.

In self-defence she began to babble that Ralph and Sheena had called in on a visit, that Mildred had been with her for supper, that they were going off on a holiday together, they had been making plans.

Liz set the jar of coffee down. "You mean you're going away?"

"Yes."

"When?"

"As soon as we can get bookings—almost at once."

"But you can't." Liz flamed as if she had been dipped in scalding water. "What will I do?"

"Do? Whatever do you mean?"

"I'll be alone."

"Everything will be all right. Mrs. Parsons will be in to see to things, and there's always Johnnie."

"Half the time Johnnie isn't here. It was one o'clock last night and tonight he's not home yet." (Scaring some delighted girl at ninety miles an hour?) "Do you have to go? I mean just now? I wish you hadn't."

So that's it. You've found out what desire does to you for the first time in your positive well-organised life. Sweet lust. Suddenly everything is turned upside down, your neat sanity and just causes. All you want is his body and he yours. And he comes in for coffee and because you both know that I'm downstairs in my flat the relationship is safe and enchanted, eyes and hands produce their tame ecstasies and the Passionate Preacher goes away unmolested. But if my flat is empty this house won't be safe for either of you, not any longer. And you're afraid.

"This is a pleasant time of year to go, I think the change will do me good. Mildred is so excited about it, I wish you'd seen her."

The girl's face thickened. Julia remembered that look of sullen panic. ("No, I can't stay any longer but the bedroom door is open, the light is burning on the landing, you have said your prayers and done your teeth, the wardrobe is fastened and won't swing open, and your homework is finished. Now I'm going downstairs to finish my sewing, and if you call I will hear you.")

"We should get away early next week," she said.

165

"Oh. All right. I suppose so," Liz said, backing towards the door.

"Wait, Liz—you've forgotten the coffee."

Liz grabbed the jar and bolted.

Around midnight she heard Johnnie's car but no voices; he had come home alone. Then music from his flat, not the radio. He was playing his old school recorder. "Au Clair de la Lune" over and over. She closed the window in order to avoid hearing it.

Much later her phone rang. Already on the edge of sleep she groped for the receiver. At first no one spoke. Then "Julia —is that you, Julia?"

"Oh. Madge. I didn't recognise your voice. It doesn't sound like you. Is anything the matter?"

"I wanted to know if I could come round."

"Now? Isn't it getting rather late?"

"Is it? I don't know what the time is."

"Are you sure you're all right?"

"Of course I'm all right, don't be idiotic."

"Your voice sounded odd."

"I want to tell you something, Julia." The voice still sounded odd, slurred but emphatic. "When you asked me to go with you today—I could have gone."

"My dear, don't worry. I understood. In any case Mildred came."

There was silence, she thought Madge had hung up. Then Madge said "So I thought if I came round and talked to you and tried to explain."

I know what you mean by that and I can't bear it, not on

166

top of everything that has happened today. I'm tired, Madge, drained, done out. I don't want you to come and let down your hair and expect me to let down mine. I know what you'll say and how you'll say it, by fits and starts, with wet eyes and a flushed face, your hands wrenching at your shoulder-straps or twisting a rag of a handkerchief. Things aren't the same as they used to be, you'll say. I have been cold and peculiar to you, you don't know what you've done, it must be your fault, won't I tell you? I don't want to go through all this, Madge, I'm getting too old for this kind of emotional wallow, it's time you were. Either I shall sit and listen and mock you privately and hate myself for doing this, or else—and this is frightening because it could happen—I'll grab hold of you, Madge, my dear Madge, using your love to fill the gaps that I've made by opting out of other loves that don't work any more, and the independence that that idiot Mildred and I have almost achieved will go down the drain. You've come too late. I'm going away with Mildred because she doesn't matter to me very much and it will be bliss to be with someone who doesn't matter. You still matter though I won't tell you this, but you can't make claims on me now. Nor will I listen to the inevitable lament for Harold that is sure to follow—I will not be bound to you by my dead husband. In any case your Harold isn't mine. You dote on a man who never grew up, never really existed. You didn't know the man I loved and lived with and whose children I bore and whose body was as familiar to me as my food. I knew everything about him, every little thing, glorious and inglorious. There isn't any way of telling you this and even if there was I wouldn't tell you.

We must mourn him in our separate ways, it's only decent. Even if you need help I won't exchange my dead husband for your stained-glass hero. I can't do that, Madge. And I'm afraid I might be tempted to try because you can create immortality for your Harold, but mine is dead already.

"Julia. Are you listening? Please let me come."

"Madge dear, I'm sorry but it's late and I really am tired. Surely tomorrow would do?"

Only Madge's broken breathing replied. Julia said "I've had a confusing kind of day. The children have been here and Mildred stayed for supper—"

"Mildred?"

"I told you she came with me when you couldn't come; we were having a little celebration."

"Celebration?"

That was a mistake. Now I must explain to her why I was having a celebration with Mildred when we had come back from a visit to my husband's grave. "We're planning to go off on a holiday, Mildred and I. The children think it would be good for me to get away for a while. Suppose you and I have lunch tomorrow, I'll tell you about it."

"Not tomorrow. I can't."

"As soon as we can fix it then, Madge," Julia said pressing on wearily. "I'm sorry Madge—about tonight, I mean."

"I'm sorry. I shouldn't have asked."

We shall go on and on being sorry and achieving nothing. She was terrified now that Madge was weeping.

"Madge—you do understand. Madge?"

After a moment she heard Madge say: "Of course. Of

course it's too late. I've no right to bother you." Her voice was discordantly loud, the words jarred. "But I wanted to tell you —I went up there this evening after you'd been. Your daffodils had toppled over and I straightened them. I thought you'd like to know." And she rang off.

CHAPTER TEN

"Ah good morning, Madam, your bookings have just come through." The young man behind the counter beamed. (He remembers our babbling enthusiasm, he's getting his babble in first to show that he is tuned in.) "Well, you were lucky, Madam. I said at the time you might be and you were, a couple of cancellations just in time for us to snap them up—the very hotel we recommended—you'll find it all here." He slapped a sheaf of papers in front of her.

"I'm sorry. We're not going after all. I'm afraid you'll have to cancel everything."

"Madam?"

"We've had a change of plans."

"Ah, I see." He looked pained and made a note on a slip of paper which he added to the sheaf, then snapped a rubber band round them. "You've decided to go somewhere else?"

"Yes. Ireland."

"Ah—Ireland?" He brightened and tuned in to the Emerald Isle. "Ireland of the Welcomes, the Land of Saints and Scholars, a broth of a country as they say. You'll like Ireland and the Irish, Mrs.—Stevens." Shamrocks sprouted invisibly under his fingers. "It rains, of course, that's why it's so green." He invited her to share the joke about the Irish weather and became engrossed with more leaflets. "Now let me see. A flight to Dublin—you'll need a couple of days there—the

Book of Kells, Trinity College, the Phoenix Park and the tomb of Jonathan Swift. Isn't it a pity now you're too late for the Nelson pillar?" His voice warmed and took on a matey roundness with a thickening of the "t's" and the "r's" delayed and tucked`under the tongue. Her armour of Ulster prickles rose and she stared at him stonily, despising the English who are such easy victims to the charms of Ireland. This was quite a pleasant sensation—years since she'd felt it.

The young man didn't notice the danger signal, he had ticked off Glendalough, Killarney, Cork (Blarney Castle a "must") and the house of Sir Philip Sidney at Youghal with the Faerie Queene hovering somewhere around, and he was scampering round the Ring of Kerry before she interrupted.

"Northern Ireland."

"I beg your pardon?"

"Ulster. The Black North."

"Ah." He changed into the less familiar, more elusive key. The Glens of Antrim, the Coast Road, the Mountains of Mourne sweeping down to the Sea, the Giant's Causeway rising up out of it, the walled city of Londonderry (Cecil Frances Alexander and the siege where they ate rats) and the white lonely beaches of Donegal (homespun tweeds) only a few miles across the Border. An easy flight to Aldergrove—

"No thank you," Julia said, "I want a corner seat reservation facing the engine on the boat train from Euston to Liverpool, near the dining-car, a second class return ticket with

171

a Saloon ticket on the Belfast boat and a single cabin, 'B' deck
if possible—"

"That would be two single cabins, Madam?"

"One," she told him. "I'm going alone."

I am going alone because there is no one to go with me and
in any case I choose to be alone. It may be a choice of necessity
but all the same it is a choice. There isn't anyone I would want
to take with me. This isn't a flight, it's a mission, a pilgrimage
maybe. (Shall I tell him that? It would please him—the returning Irish exile in search of the ancestral four whitewashed
walls.) I am in fact in search of myself. (That sounds sufficiently
ham to appeal to him, but it is true.) For so long I have been
tangled with other people, out of love, duty, necessity, habit.
My duty now is to give them back the responsibility I have
assumed for them. I have come out at the other end of the
tunnel.

I want to be able to see again with a single and undistracted
eye, not a multiple vision from which I must work out an
average. (If the family were with me now Harold would be
passing the ball of affability back to this young man, playing
the game a little heavily, Ralph would have discovered some
error in his planning and have put him right, Liz would
criticise him for his smoothness, Johnnie would suspect me of
falling for it, Sheena wouldn't be registering at all because her
breasts are heavy and she must get back for the next feed, and
I would be involved in all these attitudes and confused by
them.) I'm tired of adjusting myself to other people and blaming myself because I notice the adjustments they make to me.
I'm tired of watching my reflection in other people's mirrors.

I am, of course, to blame for this habit of watching myself; Lionel was right, I want too many people to love me.

I want this more since Harold died, you become accustomed to being loved. Harold loved me steadfastly—habitually perhaps. But all my concerns were his, no experience was ever single, there was always Harold. I don't know how long the first enchantment lasted with him—I'd like to think it lasted longer with him than it did with me but I can't honestly be sure. There was a moment somewhere when ardour became loyalty, I didn't spot it, and in any case I didn't mind. I liked Harold better loyal than ardent, he was never much at home with ardour and I'd had plenty of it in Ireland before Harold. The Irish are great lovers, I wonder this young man didn't mention it—great verbal lovers, I mean; we have to talk about something during the long Celtic twilight and we don't make love except in the dark, and we are afraid of the dark anyway.

So I am going back to Ireland. I want to see things again with the honest eye of my childhood. I want to shed prejudices, my own and other people's. I am tired of trying to be mature and only being empty and trivial. I am tired of playing small. I want to be purged of levity and sourness. I want to rid myself of the habit of gentle mockery which affords me a certain kind of protection, the habit of not expecting too much so that I won't be disappointed. I am going back to Ireland to expect everything.

I want to be moved again against sense or reason. I want to be amazed by sunsets and made to weep by things like poverty and love. I want to stare at children's faces with awe. I'm not out to hunt for leprechauns at the bottom of anyone's garden, heaven forbid, but I demand the right to be devastated by any and all of the simple primitive emotions.

I was born in Ireland and bred there, my roots are there. I don't expect to enjoy my return, I still feel the impatient critical love for the place that I did when I left it, but it is the right place for my purpose. I will visit people who knew me as a child and whom I knew as children. I will be stripped of everything that adult experience has given me to protect myself with. There is terror and honesty in childhood resought. I am not being maudlin or masochistic. If this turns out to be a ridiculous performance I am prepared to be ridiculous.

I need to do this because it will not be long before I grow into an old woman. I may live to be a very old woman in whom bodily shame has already died and there is no grace left. I won't take kindly to old age, but when I am old I must have something inviolable in myself to hold on to, something peculiar to me. This is what I am looking for.

"You'll like the Irish," the young man said.

"I do," she told him, but kindly, "I'm Irish myself."

On the way from the Travel Agency she tried to phone Madge to fix a date for lunch but there was no reply. There had been no reply in the morning either, or yesterday. On an impulse she rang Lionel at his office.

"Good morning, Julia."

"I've been trying all day to get through to Madge but there wasn't any reply. Yesterday too. She can't be out all the time, can she?"

"It seems unlikely." He sounded brusque, she must have got him at an awkward moment.

"I wanted to arrange for us to have lunch together before I went away."

"Are you going? I didn't know."

"To Ireland."

"Ah—the scenes of your youth."

"And all that," she said, denying him the right to be amused, "staying with Charles."

"Good," he said.

"Lionel, is Madge all right? I mean do you know if anything's the matter?"

"My dear Julia why should there be?"

"She rang me a couple of nights ago, she sounded very depressed. She asked if she could come round and talk but I put her off, it was after midnight."

"You know what Madge is—she never learned to read a clock. What did she want to talk about?"

"I think it was Harold."

"You go to Ireland," he said, "I'll look after Madge."

"I feel responsible, perhaps there's something I could do."

"Why should you feel responsible?"

How can I say "Because she loves me." Lionel ought to know. She said "Oh all right then Lionel," and rang off, feeling dissatisfied.

She walked through the park to reach Mildred's house. It was a fine spring evening of newly extended light, with pale nets stretched over the almond trees and the branches of the cherries armed to their tips with buds. The symbolism was aggressively obvious, it didn't do anything to her, she wasn't fooled, Harold was dead, there was nothing new to discover, only the seasons repeat. The first of the year's lovers were linking along below the trees. She watched them. This is what is wrong with me. I have forgotten how to be moved. If this journey is going to succeed then I must let the spring—and anything else—make a fool of me.

Cora came to open the door. She looked frightened. Mother was upstairs with Daddy. She was with him all the time. The doctor had been again this morning, he said Daddy was a little better. Mother was marvellous. "I don't know how she does it," Cora said, "I didn't know it could be like this." She gulped and said she would tell her mother that Julia was there.

She returned in a few moments and asked Julia to go upstairs.

"Are you sure it's all right."

"She says it is."

"Are you coming?"

"I can't bear it," Cora cried, "I daresay you think I'm awful, but I can't."

Mildred was standing at the door of the bedroom waiting for her. "Julia my dear, how lovely of you to come!"

"Mildred!" It was all very formal. She didn't remember having kissed Mildred before but Mildred offered herself. "Come in," she said.

"He isn't sleeping, is he?"

Mildred said she didn't think so, he would think it was lovely of her to come.

They sat on chairs on opposite sides of the bed in the darkened room. It was just possible to see the shape of Wilfred propped low on pillows. Julia asked "How are you today, Wilfred?" "Daddy says the doctor thinks there's quite an improvement today," Mildred interpreted. Wilfred didn't move or speak. "Stuffed full of sedatives, poor old Daddy, but he knows it's for the best," Mildred explained.

"Is his speech—?"

"Just for the moment, we hope. The doctor says it should come back gradually—partially in any case—that's right, isn't it?" She lifted Wilfred's hand from the counterpane and folded it between both of hers. Julia's eyes were becoming accustomed to the limited light. Mildred held herself like a queen. She patted her husband's hand. "Well, this is nice, isn't it? Now Julia, we want to hear all your news."

Julia told her of the planned journey to Ireland. She nodded and smiled. "That will be nice, Julia; it will do you good. You'll send us a postcard, won't you?"

"Oh Millie! Our lovely holiday."

"It was a mad idea, we were crazy," Mildred said, "how I ever imagined I could get away."

"He took ill at the office, didn't he?"

"Actually between ourselves it was at a matinee in a cinema —one of his hunting grounds, it seems. The management had their eye on him—that was why they noticed at once when he slumped."

"How long does the doctor think?"

"Slow. It's bound to be slow, isn't it, Daddy?"

"You're going to need help—a nurse—"

"Later on perhaps. Just now he likes me to do everything for him—don't you?"

Across Wilfred's dulled face—the mouth pulled to one side, the eyelids drooping—something flickered that could have been entreaty, or thanksgiving, or even a sexy leer.

"But the nights—"

"I could always do on very little sleep."

"You'll be worn out, Mildred."

"Daddy's very good, no trouble at all. And the girls are doing everything they can."

After a few minutes Julia rose to go. Her holiday plans, her health, her very mobility were an embarrassment.

Mildred came to the door with her. "I hope you have a simply lovely time. I won't come downstairs with you if you don't mind—he doesn't like me to go away." The eyes of the man in the bed had moved and were watching her.

"Mildred—I hate leaving you like this—if you have one of your headaches—"

"I shan't," Mildred said, "and would you tell Cora on your way out that Daddy and I are ready for a nice cup of tea." Before Julia left she watched her returning to the side of the bed with an expression of the most profound content. Julia went downstairs feeling muddled and humble and grateful that Harold had not been the man in the bed.

On Friday Johnnie announced that he would drive his mother to the station. He drove with more than his usual exuberance but she didn't remonstrate being wholly occupied in silent prayer, and they arrived safely. He found her carriage which was empty, and bought her an extravagant number of glossy magazines.

"Go on now, Johnnie. Don't wait. I hate being seen off."

"Are your frightened of a long embarrassing tongue-tied farewell?"

"That's right," she laughed, "do go."

He got into the carriage and sat beside her, fidgeting with the strap of the window. She wished he would leave her. "Ten minutes to make small earnest conversation," he said, and made it. Then "Give Uncle Charles my respects; tell him I'm following the bachelor tradition."

"I will."

"You'll be all right over there, won't you?"

"Of course I will."

"By yourself, I mean."

Further up the platform doors were slammed. She said "We're going now."

He kissed her quick and hard and got out. "Enjoy yourself. Have a lovely nostalgic time. Don't think about us, will you?"

"I won't," she said sternly and drew up the window, making a business of fastening it, so that by the time it was done and she had lifted her head he was already out of sight.

She sat back in her corner, triumphant but a little lonely, because Harold should have been in the corner opposite, their knees touching, his eyes making more firm, more valid, her image of herself embarked on this journey, and asking, as always for the confirmation of love. The need to respond to him rose in her, and died, sickeningly. The walls and back yards and parks and tunnels and flats and factories and suburban stations of London ran away from her, and she fixed her attention on the label on her suitcase—"Mrs. Julia Stevens, Belfast via Liverpool".

CHAPTER ELEVEN

"Julia!" they cried with delight, "Julia Moore! How wonderful to see you! It's been years and years!"

"I simply couldn't believe it when Diana rang up and said you were on this side of the water—"

"Julia—you haven't changed a scrap!"

"Of course I've changed!"

"The same, the very same!"

"And I said to Diana 'By this time she'll be terribly, horribly English—you wait!' "

So they still do it, do they—suspect anyone of treachery who leaves Ireland and transplants successfully, assume a phoney native roughness at the first suspected whiff of polish from across the water, still throw out graces with airs, justify themselves with the same aggressive humility by insisting on the English demand for superiority even though it may not be made. Diana's drawing-room was full of half-recognised middle-aged ladies crowding round her. She smiled and listened to their welcome and their names, trying to see behind their faces—God, are we all as old as that, how do we endure it?—the faces of the girls she used to know, and wondering how much of young Julia Moore they really found in her. But she was grateful for the warmth in their voices and listened privately to her own voice in case it might sound clipped and English. She broadened her vowels a trifle for courtesy's sake. The fact that these women had known her as a child, a girl, filled her with clearest joy.

"What in the world brings you back to Belfast?" they demanded, condemning her for ever having found it possible to go away. "What are you doing here?" insisting that no one in their senses would make the return journey voluntarily. She remembered the traditional attitudes and loved them willingly.

Charles had asked much the same when he brought her home for breakfast on the morning of her arrival. He still lived in the plain square house on the Loughside where they had been born. "I don't know what you're going to find to do with yourself over here, Judy, you're bound to be dull." No romanticism, please; we love Ireland passionately and privately, we don't want any song and dance.

Not dull. Nothing about it could be dull. After the journey north and the crossing—the stewardess has an Irish tongue, the boat is lifting a little, we are coming round the Isle of Man—and the exhilaration of standing on the deck as they came up the Lough in the chill of early morning, purple water, green fields, blue hills, the shape of the Cave Hill remembered a moment before it is seen and coming home to her heart like a bird, the grey sky paling to luminous northern daylight, the houses on the shore watching for her, the gantries, chimneys, steeples, the water calm now, thick like oil with the boat carving its passage through it, the stir on the quayside, the boat shuddering as the rhythm of the engines changed, then the first sight of Charles, and the shock because, seeing him before he had seen her he looked so like Father;

the drive through familiar streets of the city, the new tall flat-faced buildings ("What do you think of our shoe-boxes?" from Charles, forbidding her to despise them because they showed that his city thrived), the suburbs reached, buildings thinning, now the last turning, the gate, the drive, the house in rapid crescendo—she was at the mercy of every object remembered or suddenly recollected.

"I'm home," she said, standing in the middle of the large hall, light-headed with tiredness and excitement. "I've come home."

"Everything is the same, you haven't changed a thing," she declared as breakfast was ending—china, silver, cutlery had each given her their welcome—"not a thing, Charles." Charles folding his napkin meticulously looked at her with a trace of alarm, in case there might be anything she wanted to change, or as if he feared the returning emigrant's enthusiasm would threaten by dramatisation the integrity of the familiar things that were part of himself.

If anything had changed it was Charles, this grey, staid, attentive brother. On home ground the change was startling. Charles had been the rebel, the scoffer, the mocker of parental authority, of his inherited provincialism and Protestant persuasion. Deliberately wild and loud, he had railed against the Establishment, he had friends who were of the Roman faith. Against all expectation he settled down in the family business when war was over. What had happened to his style and gaiety? She came into the hall and watched him while he brushed his hat and compared his wrist-watch with the clock that had always been his enemy.

"It still keeps good time?"

"Of course." Again the look of alarm.

All right, all right, I am your sentimental sister from England taking an extravagant nostalgic journey into the days that are gone, you must suffer me. If the children could see me now it would slay them, but I am not defending myself against anything, this is part of the reason why I have come. I am making myself deliberately vulnerable.

"Father took it as a personal insult when that clock lost time," she said.

"Did he?"

"You must remember. It was always a joke." Anything for which Charles could mock his father must be remembered, but he fumbled unsuccessfully in the past and said: "There's no point in a clock that doesn't keep time. Judy, I've a couple of appointments this afternoon, I won't be back until dinner. I'm sorry but that's the way of it, I don't know what you'll do with yourself. There's the telly, of course—I don't know if you care for that sort of rubbish."

"Don't worry, I'll find plenty to occupy myself. You mustn't feel you have to entertain me as if I was a visitor, Charles."

"No, of course not." He smiled at her shyly, rubbing his hand up the back of his head. "It's just that I don't want you to be dull."

"I won't."

"Lunch," he fussed, "about lunch. I think Mrs. Lennon makes herself a snack before she goes home, but I don't suppose it's up to much."

184

"I'll get myself something after she's gone."

"You could come and have lunch with me in the Club."

"Oh, I don't know. I'd rather stay here. I want to mooch about."

"Do you? Mooch?" He made it sound indecent, mooching with intent. "I'll see you at dinner then."

"What happens about dinner? Can I do anything?"

"Mrs. Lennon comes in for an hour."

"You seem to have got hold of a treasure, Charles."

"She does well enough."

"All the same I wish it was Hannah in the kitchen."

"Hannah was past it, you know she was. Mad as a hatter. Once Father had gone—"

"I still wish it was Hannah."

He looked at her reprovingly and said "Mrs. Lennon will give you a much better meal. But I don't know how you're going to put in the rest of the day."

"Wandering—looking at things—"

"I hope you haven't been letting yourself get morbid, Judy, it doesn't do," he said in a grieved voice.

"Of course I haven't. Anyhow I'll probably ring Diana."

"Diana?"

"Diana Boyd. You remember. We were at school."

"You can't expect me to remember all the girls you were at school with."

"But surely—Diana—weren't you at Queen's with her brother?"

"Oh, you mean Reggie—a carroty-haired sort of fellow?"

"No. You're thinking of Reggie Baird."

"Baird? Was it Baird? That's right—Baird. One of the Bairds of Drumglass."

"What happened to Reggie Baird?"

This time Charles knew. "He was killed—shot down over France, poor devil."

Enter suddenly Reggie Baird, sweatily magnificent in flannels, in a summer shrubbery at a garden fete (he was running the coconut shies) becoming ardently and unexpectedly poetic to the smell of the hot laurels, with the sun dappling his hands and turning the short hairs on his forearms and on the area of his chest which his open neck exposed to rich threads of gold. Exit Reggie burning in mid-air, dropping while he died, this time the aim has been accurate. One ought to have been told these things. Otherwise experience is incomplete and memory a cheat.

"I didn't know you kept up with anyone over here," Charles said. Pity our provincialism, our little world that you opted out of, if you dare.

She skipped this and said: "But Diana was my best friend, we never missed a Christmas."

Thirty-five Christmas cards and a telephone call later Diana was astounded—delighted—to learn that Julia was back in Belfast. She must come round tomorrow afternoon—not a day must be lost, she would tell the others, they would be thrilled.

The first morning was spent reclaiming territory, seeing, recognising, touching, idling through the large plain rooms full of her childhood, the pictures, the ornaments, and then the garden with the Lough water spread at the foot of it; the

186

leaves and flowers a month behind the English spring, giving a sense of time arrested, youth reclaimed. She was aware of Mrs. Lennon discreetly busy by the evidence of a flapping duster, a step on the stairs, a door that closed quietly at the end of a passage. Once she saw her stooping in the kitchen garden, once they met on the stairs and exchanged greetings.

By midday she was sated and lay down on the bed, her own bed, and fell asleep and recognised at once on waking by the angle and texture of the sunlight that it was mid-afternoon, and fell asleep again from peaceful pleasure.

When she woke again the room was shadowy, light fading, the sky big with clouds. Twilight, the sad delicious shivering time, the time when you leaned on the window-sill and felt your body stir and wondered what was going to happen to you when you grew up. She rose quickly and looked at her face in the mirror and the room watched her and was amused. Momentarily she panicked, but there was Mrs. Lennon, head bent and a decent dark coat around her, speeding up the gravel to prepare Charles' evening meal.

It was a good meal as Charles had promised. Afterwards in the morning-room (the drawing-room is still for Sundays) Charles in his father's chair with the newspaper, she flipping through a magazine, her sense of peace and identification returned. We are children again, playing house together, the Father and Mother game that we used to play.

Mrs. Lennon came to the door with her coat on to say: "I'm away now, Mr. Charles." She looked at him with the dark tender eyes of a dog. "Thank you, Mrs. Lennon," Charles said, "tomorrow, then." He folded his paper across, shook it, laid it on his knee and picked it up again.

"Father used to do that."

"Do what?"

She said "It doesn't matter." His problems are over, he has solved them all by going back into the womb.

"Are you tired, Judy?"

"No. It's been a lovely day."

"It isn't going to be very lively for you here."

"I don't expect it to be."

He looked at her as if he only half believed her and asked how Lionel was and Mildred, making a creaking effort to be interested in these names that were her friends. "And that Valkyrie woman, I can't remember what she's called."

"You mean Madge?"

"Do I? She was Lionel's sister."

"That's right. How clever of you, Charles. You only saw her at the wedding and the funeral." She gave him news of them and he went back to his paper. One by one the cross-Channel boats passed down the Lough.

So next afternoon to Diana's to meet the girls, Diana so unchanged one wanted to cry. As she had promised the girls were thrilled. "Such a long, long time, Julia! You never came back."

She murmured reasons that seemed to her thin, but they were accepted with charity.

"How's that gorgeous English husband of yours?"

Daggers from Diana who had been careful to pass the word around in case somebody mightn't have heard, and her message hadn't reached the person who needed it. An empty moment before Julia said: "My husband died suddenly in November, but I don't see how you could have known."

"My dear, I am so terribly sorry—"

"Please—please—!"

Pity for each other's embarrassment sprang and collided and returned to its source. How terrible for her not knowing (and yet she ought to have known). How awful of me (and yet when she stays away so long she really can't expect—).

"Herbert was such a lamb," someone said.

"Harold," she murmured but didn't press the point.

They said: "Now tell us about your clever family," moving with relief to firmer ground. Diana's daughter, a tender nymph-like creature, came to help with the teacups. "Your family!" they demanded. She made amusing caricatures of Ralph, Sheena, Johnnie, distant precious people from whom she was now almost totally detache d. "And then there's Liz, the baby—she was born slap in the middle of an air-raid."

"The war!" they cried, "the raids, the black-out!" They told her about the bombing in Belfast in case she hadn't heard about it. They swapped and aired domestic epics. Julia won hands down when it came to rationing, the others were guiltily conscious how convenient the Border had been, how good the steaks in Dublin.

"Now tell me about yourselves," and they told her, jobs, marriages (husbands dealt with quickly in deference to her widowhood), births, illnesses and sorrows, their elderly parents, the menopause, their travels, their children's careers, their own charitable activities, their busy lives, items of local news ("You must have heard!" "My dears, you know the English papers don't print any Irish news unless it's a riot!") and for a while she listened. A suspicion of glazed inattention drove them to further efforts. They had the disadvantage of being tied tightly to truth, being in the middle of a host of witnesses, and they envied Julia her freedom of interpretation. The party was sagging, something had to be done. Diana rummaged in a drawer and produced a school photograph in which Julia had no advantage over the rest of them.

They examined their smooth flat faces as if there should be some secret hidden in them. "There you are, Julia. You were such a pretty little thing. Always so good."

"Good? Was I? I'm sure I wasn't."

They insisted she had been good. Seven-year-old Julia looked smugly from the photograph. "I simply can't imagine you grown-up and married and a grandmother," they cried. Their own ageing was more credible since Julia Moore had undergone a similar experience and reached much the same destination. It helped them. Girlhood wasn't altogether a figment of the imagination, nor middle-age a fault.

They talked of days in the Junior School with special emphasis on the things Julia had done or said, many of which seemed to her unlikely and unfamiliar. I wasn't like that. That was somebody else. Or do we only exist in the interpretation other people put on us, two dozen little Julia Moores all different? Without any warning a sudden sick ache for Harold, for steadfastness, quickly stifled. "What horrible little animals we were." They spoke of self knowledge growing, fostered by Miss Jones (Cynthia) the young Art Mistress, Cynthia sitting down beside them at the desk, squeezing close (spongecloth and slave bangles) turning her soft brown eyes and saying "Now—let's begin, shall we?" and the fluttering excitement at the thought that experience shared could be infinitely richer than the single world of oneself.

"I must go," she said at last, "I really must."

"Where are you staying?"

"With Charles, my brother."

"Ah, of course. Quite a public figure, we're always hearing him on radio and seeing his photo in the papers. He never married, did he?"

She told Charles about it in the evening. It was chilly, she must have grown soft living in the South of England, she fetched a warmer cardigan. She saw that there was a jar of half opened daffodil buds on the mantelpiece, striped green and yellow like an assembly of Elizabethan doublets, armed with spears of blue-green leaves.

Mrs. Lennon knocked and announced her departure. "If that's everything, Mr. Charles." "Thank you, Mrs. Lennon." He shook his paper and turned it on his knee. She withdrew, closing the door softly.

She went with Charles to the church on Sunday, in a hat

that earned his silent approval. The church was full, all the women wore hats. She knelt and found the God of her childhood waiting for her, Gentle Jesus, the Tender Shepherd. I have no simplicity now for which I must ask His pity. Pity my confusion, my lack of direction, the tangle of my dispersed affections, my concern with small things, my petty clevernesses, my cowardice and self-indulgence. Pity me because I have found out that the answers are not all in the book. Why didn't You tell me that love was never simple or necessarily enjoyable?

During the next week she took buses into the countryside and found it as beautiful as she remembered, but unsatisfying and irrelevant. The mountains offered no assurance, the glens no comfort, it had nothing to do with her. She came back tired and dazed and empty and told Charles in the evenings where she had been and how lovely it was.

"I saw our cottage at Cushendun today, Charles. Do you remember that holiday?"

"Only vaguely."

"You must, you must."

"Why must I?" he asked, patiently amused.

The white crescent of sand, the scooped slopes of the sandhills pierced with rushes, the presence of Scotland across the water, how can you not remember?

"That was the holiday we had Rufus," Charles said.

"Scamp, wasn't it?"

"No, Rufus. He used to chase seagulls, silly ass."

It doesn't matter which dog it was. There is no shared re-entry into childhood, it was a separate experience for each of us, we can't hope to explore it together in retrospect and discover anything new.

"And Father fished—or thought he fished. He was always so terribly anxious to be matey with the locals, don't you remember, Charles? I used to be ashamed in case they were laughing at him privately."

"He always made friends easily," Charles said.

She was annoyed and said "Not like Mother."

"Mother was shy."

"Or frigid," she said, "I often wondered. Didn't you?"

He didn't answer. His bulk seemed to grow darker—they had not yet turned on the light—and she realised her question had been offensive and that she had intended it to be. At the bottom of the garden the Lough moved restlessly. She ached for Charles to understand.

"Charles, they were real people. They're dead now."

"They were our parents," he said from his seat at the other side of the unkindled fire. It is no use. We may play the Father and Mother game, but even though we are now adults we mustn't violate the temple of parenthood.

Mrs. Lennon came in to say goodnight. Julia imagined that she lingered. "I'm away now, Mr. Charles," with the same significant patience. "Very well, Mrs. Lennon. Goodnight." In the glance they exchanged there was no mistaking their passionate rectitude, their propriety, their pleasure in discipline and in the pain that this woman and her brother inflicted on each other.

Next day another reunion party. It was bright and sunny, warm enough for her to go without her coat. "Julia!" they greeted her, "fancy you—out in your figure!" She laughed and said: "I haven't heard anyone say that for years!" And they became at once self-conscious, as if their use of the local phrase was somehow vulgar. "How English you've grown!" they teased.

The parties in any case had begun to tire. All that could be found to be said had been said long ago, but the impulse to hospitality must be sated. They rummaged in their memories to find more to say, lapsed into current domestic issues that she knew nothing about and returned painstakingly to Julia and the things she knew. And at the end of this party as at the end of the others the familiar cry. "Just the same, Julia! You haven't changed a scrap!"

She walked home with the tears streaming down her face, lonelier than she had been. Not changed? What do you know about me? Of course I have changed. The Liverpool boat was slipping down the Channel. Harold, she cried, Harold, Harold, Harold.

The telegram was waiting on the hall table where Mrs. Lennon had left it. It was from Liz and read: "You couldn't come home, could you?"

After dinner she told Charles: "I think I should go back tomorrow, Charles."

"I was afraid you'd find it dull, Judy."

"No. Not dull."

Mrs. Lennon knocked and came in. "My sister is leaving us tomorrow, Mrs. Lennon."

"Yes, Mr. Charles," and when the door closed the sound of her feet down the kitchen passage was like the beat of wings.

CHAPTER TWELVE

"I just thought you should be here," Liz said, "in case there was anything that ought to be done."

"About what? You haven't told me yet." She was tired, nervous, the automatic impulse of concern seemed to be rusty. What is all this? Why do I have to come rushing back to pick up the pieces? You're a big girl now. Is this some kind of contrived drama—

"You'll have to tell me about it, dear," she said, brightly.

"That's what I'm trying to do." Liz looked pinched and pale as if she had a bad taste in her mouth. Plainly this wasn't a girl who had been ravished in her bed-sitter when she didn't intend to be, or one who has knelt with wild declarations to embrace a man's knees and he has simply kicked himself loose and gone home. But everything about Julia's return had been unexpected.

Johnnie met her at the station with a closed look on his face. The shop he said was taking care of itself this afternoon. They would need a taxi, his car was laid up, no not what you'd call an accident.

In the taxi she asked: "Was anyone hurt, Johnnie?"

"A girl who was with me took a bit of a knock."

"Was she anyone I know?"

"The nice girl," he said, making a small sour joke of it, "you remember."

"Is it serious?"

"I don't know yet, the hospitals don't tell you much. For God's sake, Mum, don't go on, it was Liz who sent the S O S, nothing to do with me." They finished the journey in miserable silence, elbow to elbow.

Liz had stayed home from the office, that meant it was serious. "What is it, Liz? Come on, dear, you'll have to tell me."

Liz pushed a cup of instant coffee at her. "I don't suppose you had any lunch."

Julia waited and finally said "Why did you think I should be here? Tell me, Liz. What's wrong?"

Liz screwed the top back on the coffee jar meticulously. At last she said "If you want to know it was Madge."

"Madge?"

The girl sat down suddenly, gripping the table's edge and trembled as if she were fighting acute nausea.

"Has something happened to Madge?"

"It was terrible! If you'd been here to see her—it was disgusting!"

"You'd better drink this yourself." Julia pushed the cup back to her. "Come on."

Liz shook her bent head. "It would make me sick." The cup sat between them on the table, cooling.

"You're behaving like a child."

"I know. I know."

And I know what to do with a child who has the unspeakable thing locked inside them. I must help you to tell me. I'll begin by guessing. It was the dribbling imbecile girl who pushed her face at you as you were coming home from school, or shame at the lie you told and that has been found out, or the sad atrocious story that jumped out at you from the page of some man's newspaper in the bus, or the man himself who leered and touched your body as you went past.

"What about Madge? Come on—what happened? What has she done? If you don't tell me I'll go back to the station and get on with my holiday, there's still time to catch the boat train, or I'll ring Madge up and ask her to tell me." The familiar bullying routine came easily enough.

"No, no!"

"Well then—"

Liz swallowed and said "Three nights ago she came round here. We were having supper, William was here. I heard your bell ringing but I didn't bother at first. It went on ringing. It rang and rang. Then she began to shout—"

"Madge?"

"We didn't know who it was. She was shouting and hammering on the door, it was horrible. We went to see." Liz dried up again.

"You'll have to tell me."

Liz turned her face away and began to talk quickly. "When we opened the door we thought at first there was no one there, and then we looked and we saw her. It was pouring. She must have slipped on the steps and she was trying to crawl up them again on her hands and knees, but she couldn't do it very well, she kept slipping back—"

"You mean she was hurt—or ill?"

The concern in her mother's voice apparently liberated something in Liz. She laughed. "Not ill, Mum—drunk!"

197

"Drunk! Madge?"

Liz stood up and began to enjoy it. You have to suffer this because I suffered it. See how you like it. "Dead drunk, Mum —plastered. She kept on trying to get up, grabbing the steps and the wall and then falling down again, and all the time it was raining and her hands were wet and muddy and her hair was all over her face and she kept pushing it back so that she was all streaked with mud, she looked terrible, and she had that ghastly old mac on but it was flapping open and she kept treading on it and that made her fall again—"

"Surely you tried to help her?"

"She wouldn't let us. She pushed us away, the steps were slippery, she was like an animal, we couldn't get near her at first. Then she straightened up a bit and we got her as far as the porch and propped her up and she began to talk."

"What did she want?"

"You, you. Where were you, she said? Why had you gone off and deserted her?"

"I told her I was going away."

"We couldn't get any sense into her, she kept on and on. Where were you, when were you coming back, she wanted to talk to you, there was something she had to tell you, you ought to know—"

"Well—go on—did she tell you what it was?"

"I think she was going to and then—" Liz came to a full stop.

"Go on, Liz."

"I can't. She was horrible."

"All right, she was horrible. Tell me what she said."

"She steadied up and looked at William and me, and then she caught hold of his coat, to balance herself, and she laughed right in his face and asked if we were having a pleasant time. She said: 'You have to wait until she goes away, don't you? I should know.' She said a lot of other things as well, the filthiest things, I can't tell you what she said."

"All right, don't tell me. What happened after that?"

"Suddenly she let go of William and sat down on the floor in the porch and began to cry, and then she was sick and I said I'd go and ring up Cousin Lionel and tell him she wasn't well and ask him to come and fetch her home, and she said I needn't bother. 'He's gone to visit his idiot boy,' she said, 'the creature is ill and Lionel goes there every evening.'"

"What did you do?"

Liz slumped on her chair. "I should have been able to touch her, shouldn't I, Mum? I mean, even if she was foul and sick. In the office we have cases like that all the time, it's part of my job. She was just an unhappy old woman. But I felt all curled up, I couldn't do anything. I just stood there and watched her and hated her. I loathed her so much I could have spat."

"What about William? He could have done something."

"Him?" Liz began to laugh, an unpleasant croaking sound. "Well, he had his good suit on for a start. I suppose you couldn't blame him."

"What did he do?"

"I think he said 'Poor woman, poor woman,' over and over again, very pink and distressed, like the parson in a funny play. I'd never seen him like that."

"Liz. I'm sorry." Julia moved towards her but the girl went to the window and stood with her back to the room.

"Well it's better to know before you get pregnant or anything, I suppose," she said, and leaned her head against the glass and wept. When she had finished Julia asked: "What did you do with Madge in the end?"

"Waited till Johnnie came back. She got herself tidied up a bit and he took her home."

"Does Lionel know what happened?"

"I wasn't sure what to do about that. The house was empty when we got there, seething with animals of course, but Lionel wasn't home. Madge said she'd be all right and we left her, and later on I rang and Lionel was back and I told him Madge had called round and didn't seem very well, and he said he'd look in on her."

"And William?"

"I haven't a clue. That was three days ago. I haven't seen him."

"My poor Liz."

Liz put her handkerchief away. "So I thought I'd better tell you. The coffee's cold, I'm going to make some more. Then I said I'd go back to the office."

"You go ahead. I'll get anything I want."

Liz said: "Well, you know now. It isn't that I'm shocked or anything but she was beastly," and drank the cold coffee, combed her hair and fled.

When she had gone Julia rang Madge's number. She allowed it to ring for a long time. No one there, that is a good sign, it means that Madge is herself again and has gone out on a job. She hung up and gathered a scrappy lunch and carried it out to the garden, to the dusty summerhouse. A blackbird sang from a yellow jungle of forsythia. The daffodils were papery, the mouths of the exhausted crocuses had fallen apart. Summer will be upon us and something will have to be done about the garden. There is always, thank God, something that must be done. The garden is another of Harold's legacies. (Harold pottering passionately over his seed-boxes, brooding over his cuttings.) But I won't think about Harold, I will sit here and decide what plans I must make to keep the summer greenery from submerging us, what I must do about the summerhouse lacking paint and held together by dust and spiders' webs, about the litter that has accumulated here and been forgotten, the long-empty rabbit hutch, the decaying hammock, the croquet mallets (Harold's flexed wrists intent on backgarden victories) the hula hoops, the rusted roller skates. I will build a barricade of domestic trifles round me. (What do men do who are unable to protect themselves like this?) When I am ready I will think about Madge and her problems. Just now I am too busy.

Johnnie came and squatted on the floor at the entrance to the summerhouse, with his back to her. "I'm having a picnic, the first of the season," she said waving a sandwich. "Johnnie, we must make plans to clear this rubbish out."

He ignored this and asked "Did Liz tell you?"

"Yes."

"What are you going to do?"

"Go round and see Madge."

"What for?"

"I think I ought to. I tried to ring her but there was no reply. She'll be home later on."

He tore at the weeds that had grown round the doorway. After a while he said: "I got on to the hospital at last. About that girl."

"Was there any news?"

"They say she'll be all right."

"Johnnie, I am glad."

"She was pregnant, I didn't know. Anyhow she lost it."

"Johnnie."

"Go on," he said, scattering grass round him, "ask me if it was mine."

"Was it?"

"I don't know. It wasn't intended to be. I don't see it matters all that; it's just accident, isn't it—begetting? Well, isn't it?"

"Did you care for her?"

"I told you—she was a nice girl."

"But you said—"

"I know what I said. But you can't always decide beforehand who you'll go to bed with."

"What are you going to do now?"

He shrugged. "You tell me."

"Why should I? It's your life."

He put his head on his knees. "You must tell me. You've always told me. Or don't you know?"

She brushed crumbs from her skirt, finding difficulty in controlling her hands. "I'm going into the house to ring Madge again. If she's in I'm going round."

"You're eager, aren't you? What are you going to say to her?"

"I don't know. I just think she might need me."

When he turned his face shocked her. He shouted: "Exactly what did Liz tell you anyway?"

She felt a little sick. "That Madge was drunk and came round here and made a silly fuss and said that I had deserted her, and that she seemed very miserable and wretched and between you you got her home."

"Was that all?"

"She was offensive to Liz's clergyman—hinted things—"

"What sort of things? Or didn't Liz tell you?"

"Johnnie, Madge was out of her mind, she didn't know what she was saying."

"She knew all right."

"How could she? She was distracted, she would have said anything, you know how a woman talks when she's drunk. Anyway she idolised your father."

"I wasn't sure if you knew."

She laughed, feeling better. "Of course I knew. I thought everybody did, it stood out a mile. And she never tried to hide it."

"You mean you didn't mind?"

"Why should I mind? It was a kind of joke, Madge's schoolgirl crush." Comfortably secure she smiled at him. Poor silly boy.

He stood up, shutting out the afternoon sunlight. "Then I'll tell you something that isn't funny. About the last time Dad went up to London. He left his umbrella in the hall, you remember? It was raining, and I ran after him with it, and I got to the car just before they drove off."

"Careering through puddles in your pyjamas like a mad thing!"

"When I came back you said 'How was Madge?' Well I'll tell you how she was, how they both were, when I knocked on the window for them to open the door. They didn't hear me at first. They were sitting staring at each other. Their faces, like a pair of lovers on the way to bed."

She didn't speak. Johnnie's breathing fractured the blackbird's phrasing. "Somebody had to tell you. You had to know. Go on—say something."

At last she said "Was that the first time you knew?"

"I don't remember."

"You must."

"I expect I knew before. I pretended I didn't."

"Why?"

"*Why?*"

She said "I shouldn't have thought infidelity would have shocked you one way or another, Johnnie." I am doing this very well; it is extraordinary how well I am doing it.

"Listen," he said, "he was my father."

"I never knew you thought parenthood was a very significant relationship either."

He said "You win. You always have to win." After a while he groped his way towards her and put his head in her lap and cried. She gripped her hands together to prevent herself from touching him, and when he had finished crying she asked: "Who else knew?"

He stood up. "Everybody but you, I should think."

She said "I think I'll try the telephone again." He stepped aside so that she could go past without needing to touch him. The effort of walking took all her attention. He went beside her, always a little apart, making wretched movements of entreaty with his hands.

After the sun's brilliance the blackness of the house blinded her but she found the telephone. There was still no reply from Madge's number.

"No one there," she said to Johnnie's tormented face.

"What will you do now?"

"Rest for an hour or so until Lionel comes home, then I'll walk round. I'll go and sit in the park and watch the people."

"Sit in the park? You can't!" The way he said it it sounded indecent.

She said "Excuse me," absurdly, and pushed past him and fetched a coat and went down the drive and along the road to the park entrance and found an empty bench and sat there all the afternoon.

She watched the procession of prams and smiled at the young girls who pushed them and at the babies scattered like flowers over the grass, snatching at daisy heads. Their skin was still white, wanting the summer's heat. She watched the children high on the swings, the dogs and their owners, a few lovers restless and inclined to bicker because it was too early, the middle-aged couples who walked and turned and sat and rose again in unison, one mind in two bodies, not needing to speak, the solitary old men comforting themselves with their pipes, a big-bosomed woman with a spotted blouse, like a thrush (her inner arms brush against her sides as she walks, left, right, left, right, she is enjoying this); the schoolboys, some racing and whooping in gangs, and a few lone stragglers kicking their way along, heads bent, occupied in the solitary argument of childhood.

When she had gathered courage she looked up and identified beyond the trees that fringed the park the roof and gable of her own house, its chimneys and windows, realising the patterns of the curtains that were too far away to distinguish, the arrangement and function of the furniture inside each set of four walls, the shape and quality of the enclosed air, herself inside the house year after year, waiting for Harold to come home, the changing texture of her skin, her body changing inside her clothes, waiting for Harold.

The path through the park was filled with Harold returning, in all moods and seasons; jauntily in summer with bare head and his linen jacket, in winter huddled in his overcoat and limping a little because the pain was bad and the park was empty, no one there to see, strung with parcels since it was coming up to Christmas, or with a tissue cone of flowers for a celebration, importantly with exam papers for his attention, elated (from some success with Madge?) or peevishly because someone has hurt him and he needs Julia, anxious because he has remembered that one of the children is ill, or simply a tired man coming home. Harold growing older each time the leaves came down, crossing the park. The image, however it appeared, was precious and indestructible.

She didn't notice Johnnie until he was beside her and had spoken. "I thought if you were going I'd go with you." She rose and they turned together in the direction of Madge's house.

For the first time that year the city's pavements threw back warmth. The air was still heavy and she felt dazed and lethargic. Garden walls and railings were loaded with sprawling blossom, their scent came strongly.

Halfway there Johnnie said "I don't know what you're going to say to her."

"I'll know when I see her." And I know that you are afraid and yet you've begun to enjoy this because you have handed it all back to me. Mummy knows what to do about the unpleasant things of life, leave it to her, she will look after it so that it will all come right in the end.

"Come on," she said.

They turned the last corner. Lionel's car and a couple of other cars were there, but no sign of Madge's. "Lionel's home anyway."

"There seem to be some people around."

"I suppose they could be having visitors."

At some point on the pavement the smell of spring changed to that other sick crippling smell. The lower windows of the house, when they came within sight of them, were lying widely open, though the curtains had been pulled across. The curtains moved a little as the windows exhaled the bitter breath of the room into the evening.

The knot of people at the gate made no move to follow them when they turned up the drive. Madge's flower border was brilliant. The hall door lay open but the hall was empty. They hesitated. There was no welcome from the animals, none of the expected frenzy of hospitality. Somewhere there were voices.

Julia stepped into the porch and called "Is anyone at home?"

The voices stopped at once and Lionel came into the hall through a door, stepping across strips of tape that had been torn off and lay criss-crossed over the floor.

"Lionel. I came to look for Madge. And where are the animals?"

Lionel was beyond speech, but he stood aside and made a sign for her to go into the room.

CHAPTER THIRTEEN

"I can't imagine how anyone could want to die," Mildred declared. "It seems too impossible to have nothing at all to live for."

She leaned across Wilfred's body, neatly disposed and passive in the bed, to smooth an already smooth sheet. A tear splashed on to the back of Wilfred's hand and lay there, entire and bright, held in the network of veins. She saw it and mopped it with her handkerchief. "He was very upset about it," she said as if it were the man in the bed who had wept. "I thought I ought to tell him in case he overheard someone talking about her. Anyway I think he should be kept in the picture, don't you? Julia, do you think she expected to rejoin Harold?"

From her chair at the other side of the sick man Julia said "I don't know. Perhaps."

"One is bound to think about it," Mildred said.

Mildred is wrong; one isn't. This is one of the things one trains oneself not to think about. It is five months since Harold died and I am still learning the terms and nature of our separation. I can't imagine Harold disembodied and blissful; I only know the troubled man that I loved. The idea of reunion seems unnecessary, I am not yet sufficiently disengaged from him.

The bedroom radio relayed popular music. "Each little bit closer tells me something new", the singer's voice teased. "We keep it on for him most of the time," Mildred said.

"Does he really like this sort of stuff?"

"Well he can't be choosey just now, poor dear," Mildred said, smiling into her husband's vacant face, "but it's what he used to fancy. I daresay some people might think 'Abide with Me' with variations would be more suitable, but we mustn't let ourselves get dreary, must we, Daddy?"

Mildred had certainly not let herself become dreary. She looked calm, exhausted and yet inexhaustible, completely triumphant. Her face had lost all its indecision, she wore her clothes without apologising for them. Pale skin, pale clothes, flat pale hair, all lit by her own pale light.

"There was something very splendid about Madge, I always thought so," Mildred said. "She was on a different scale from the rest of us. I was sorry I couldn't come to the funeral but I knew Lionel would understand. Poor Lionel. What will he do now? I don't suppose his wife will come back to him even though Madge was the reason she left him. People always thought it was the boy but it was Madge. How did he seem when you saw him?"

"Like an old man. I only spoke a few words to him."

Even those words had not been easy to find. He said it was good of her to come, with a flat sincerity that made her breasts ache. "I wish I'd known about it sooner, Lionel. If I'd come straight round. I suppose I should have known. I think she wanted me to know, it might have helped her."

"Much better you didn't; it wouldn't have made any difference. And I wouldn't have tried to alter things, Julia. I didn't mind what she did, provided she was happy. I loved her."

Then she said "I suppose they were happy." And Lionel said:

"It was a kind of unhappy violence between them, they couldn't leave it alone, if that's any consolation to you," and turned to speak to someone else.

"Of course she may have been in the middle of her change," Mildred went on. "I mean the rest of us got it over and done with years and years ago, but Madge was the kind who would be late starting so it would probably go on longer with her, and we're supposed to do peculiar things, aren't we, though I don't think it really ever made any difference to me except that I used to get dizzy and have to come out of church, which was a bit of a bore for Daddy and the girls."

"How are the girls?"

"Wonderful, just wonderful, you wouldn't believe," Mildred said, "it's made a great difference to them, hasn't it, Daddy? We're talking about the girls, dear." She leaned forward trying to force some response from his eyes. "They simply can't do enough!" She raised Wilfred's hand and put it for a moment against her cheek, seeming to congratulate him on the improvement in their daughters, and then set it down again tidily in its place."

"Harold was God Almighty to her all her life," she went on, "it's like that with some people. Everything about him had to be absolutely perfect. That was why she was so dotty about you, I expect you guessed that—you were a side product of his glory. You had to be perfect because he would never have chosen a wife who was anything less." In the dimness of the sickroom a naive and original wisdom emanated from Mildred. "That was why she talked as if Harold and you were Great Lovers."

"Oh poor Madge."

"Love is the Sweetest Thing" the radio sobbed, picking up its cue. Mildred said "I always doted on that tune. Daddy did too." She leaned forward and spoke into his face. "The tune! That tune!"

Julia wished Mildred would switch it off. "Mildred are you sure this syrup doesn't make his head ache?"

"He likes syrup. I don't suppose Harold did."

"No."

"I wonder what he was like with Madge. You don't mind me saying that, do you dear?"

No. Unaccountably I don't. Anything can be stated in this No Man's Land with Wilfred prostrate between us. Nothing we say is vulgar or offensive even if we choose to discuss my husband and his cousin in bed. I have to think of it sometime.

"Clever men like Harold," Mildred said. "I often wonder. I expect he quoted poetry to her."

Yes, he would have done that. Donne would provide the ardour that his body might have lacked, verbal intimacy would be welcome, even if it were borrowed.

"It's surprising how sexy some poetry is," Mildred said, "the bits they used to leave out of schoolbooks but I don't suppose they do that now. Did he quote poetry to you?"

"Hardly ever." Tennyson perhaps. Browning sometimes. Certainly not Donne. It would have embarrassed him if I had appreciated it and irritated him if I hadn't. If he had had to put our relationship into literary terms he would have used Dornford Yates.

"Well, that's nice anyway," Mildred said. She rose to give

Wilfrid some fluid from a feeding-cup. "It was kind of you to come today, Julia. I remembered it was your wedding day. I thought 'I don't suppose she'll come today'. " Tenderly she wiped her husband's mouth.

"Of course I came."

"I said to him 'This is Julia's wedding day'. I thought he would be pleased to know."

"He's improving all the time isn't he?"

"Little by little. Sometimes he can make sounds."

"Oh Millie."

"No time till he's out and about again, you'll see," Mildred said.

Julia rose to go and Mildred came round the bed and embraced her. Momentarily her poise wavered and she wept.

"Oh Julia, this is what it's like, I suppose."

"I suppose so. You're wonderful, Millie."

"I'm not but this is the only way I can do it." She wiped her eyes. "We're making a collection of pot plants. He's ever so interested."

"Shall I bring him one next time I come?"

"Would you, Julia? He'd like that."

Julia went home feeling shaken and desolate. She tried to comfort herself by calling at the stationer's to buy a birthday card for Philippa, and after a search found one with a procession of quackie ducks carrying a banner with the motto "Many Happy Returns". She must remember to post it before night.

As she turned in at the gate she saw Sheena and her family on the steps. Beth and Martin were wearing schoolbags, they must have come straight from school. Sheena was unloading Philippa and the baby from the pram.

She rallied all her resources and said "My dears, what a lovely surprise!"

The children shouted and ran against her knees and Sheena said "Hallo, Mum. We just thought we'd call round for a minute on our way home."

"Come in. Come in."

She went through to the kitchen. Someone was there already. Surely Mrs. Parsons had far outstayed her time. But it was Liz who was filling the kettle. "Things were slack in the office so I took a chance and came home early. I thought perhaps you'd like tea. I brought a box of cakes."

"What a lovely idea. Sheena and the children are here."

"Are they?" Liz grumbled. "The whole circus? Now there won't be enough milk."

"Milk? Who said milk?" Johnnie had strolled in. "Hallo, Mum. Hallo, Liz. What are you doing here?"

"Making tea. But Sheena and the kids have come and they always drink pints and pints."

"I've got an overflow, I'll bring it." He went into his own flat and came back with two bottles. "Ralph's arriving with Sally-Anne, just coming up the drive. It looks like a full house."

Ralph had brought flowers. "From Sal with her love," he said, presenting them.

"They're lovely, Ralph. I'll get a vase right away."

Her hands shook as she tried to disentangle the stalks from the clinging tissue paper. So they've come, all of them. They

214

didn't arrange it among themselves or bully each other into it, they thought of it separately. They remembered the anniversary and they came to visit me in case I needed them. And I, who have trained myself not to love them too long or too much or uncritically am suddenly disarmed by love. They shouldn't do this to me, it isn't fair.

"I don't know what you've all come for," she cried. The business of arranging the flowers was impossibly laborious. Sheena said: "I'll do those. You keep Harry for me."

"He'll only cry."

"He won't."

He didn't. No one cried or had cause to cry. All the angels were on their side, all the omens were favourable. A kind of rare felicity presided over them. Johnnie was at his most gay. "Be funny, Uncle Johnnie," and he was funny. Ralph was relaxed and benevolent, his face when he turned to his mother full of unguarded affection. Liz was nimble with the teacups, chattering to Sheena and talking baby nonsense across the table to Harry. The older grandchildren were peaceable and content, ate bread and jam and cakes without greed or argument. Sally-Anne, joking with Philippa, seemed quite happy with nursery company. How pretty that girl is going to be. How good and kind they are. All this goodness and gaiety, the fruits of love. They came to restore Harold to me and they have brought their children as a guarantee against too much emotion.

"Now go into the garden and play," Sheena said when it was over. Ralph said "You too, Sally-Anne. Perhaps Aunt Sheena will allow you to wheel baby Harry." "The grass!"

Julia cried, "the grass is damp," but no one heard or heeded her. Like figures in a dream the children allowed themselves to be dispatched and were seen through the window, playing, happy and golden and slightly unfamiliar.

Left with her own children Julia said: "Well, this has been nice," and smiled at them to hide her panic. She thought she detected an air of purpose now underneath their goodwill. The occasion has become formal. They have passed the ball to me, it is my turn to play. They are waiting for me to make a statement. Don't let us have any loose ends in this family; we know about this thing that has happened. Put it right for us, kiss the hurt better. Tell us what we are to think about our father who was unfaithful to you with your friend, his cousin. When that has been done we can all go off to our separate lives.

"It was very good of you all to come," she said, "it's been a lovely party. I know your father—" "Wait for it" their faces told her—"would have appreciated it."

She looked round at them. Liz was biting her lip and twisting her fingers. Sheena had armed herself with the pretence of a piece of knitting, sometimes her eyes went to the window to make the automatic check. Johnnie had risen and was standing looking into the garden, she couldn't see his face. Ralph leaned back in his chair, a little pedantic and anxious, watching the pencil which swung like a pendulum between his finger and thumb. This is the final page in the storybook. What am I to say to you?

"I think you're waiting for me to make a speech and I don't know what to say. Sometimes I wish I'd known you all as

216

friends instead of children. It would be easier. I expect you were all shocked when you heard about Madge's death." They looked at her uneasily, hoping it was going to be all right. "You know why she killed herself. You probably knew before I did that your father and Madge were lovers. I expect you understood him better than I did because you are all like him, in your different ways."

Their faces wavered and then grew stiff.

"I don't know why that should surprise you," she said, "you are his children and children tend to be like their parents. You don't escape from him completely you know because he is dead."

"Mother—" Ralph began, half rising. Sheena had flushed brilliantly into her hair, her knitting had slipped on to the floor, Liz was shaking, Johnnie hadn't moved from his post at the window.

"Sit down, Ralph, I want to finish," she said. "After all anything that remains of your father is in you now, more than in me. And now you are all grown up and the family is finished—"

"Completed," Johnnie corrected without turning round.

"Thank you, Johnnie. 'Completed' is better. And if it is completed then why is it necessary for me to say anything to you? You can't have it both ways, you know."

"I wish you wouldn't," Liz muttered, tugging at a loose thread on the knee of her slacks. She twisted it round her finger and pulled it until it broke.

"That was silly," Julia said, "darn it from the inside and press it well and it won't show too much. I hope none of you is blaming me because Madge couldn't live without your father and I can."

None of them answered. Out in the garden the children called and laughed, running from sunlight to shadow.

"Perhaps you want me to invent some justification for your father, something trite and sentimental that you will pretend to laugh at and comfort yourselves with privately. That he never cared for Madge, that she did all the running, that he let himself be talked into it, the line of least resistance, that there was nothing in it anyway, Madge invented it all. I don't think that is true. Madge and your father loved each other from childhood, you have to accept that."

Sheena had lifted her knitting but her fingers made the tangle that she was trying to unravel more tightly knotted.

"Leave it dear, fix it later," Julia said. "Or would it help you if I said that your father and I never really loved each other, we put up politely with each other for thirty-three years and he didn't rob me of anything by his love for Madge. But that isn't true either. I think he got something from Madge that I couldn't have given him; I don't think he would have asked me for it—domestic heroics weren't really in his line, were they? Your father and I made each other happy and that is quite a rare achievement. We had a great deal to be thankful for, and I don't envy Madge anything except per- haps—" she felt them brace themselves—"her ability to use violence, yes, even in the way she died. But that wasn't what your father wanted from me. Well, was it?"

They stared, hypnotised, and shook their heads.

"He wanted me on a smaller scale, a gentler scale," she said,

218

"you all did. Small and seemly and faithful. Well, that was my line, anyway, wasn't it? I wouldn't have been any good at anything larger. But if Madge was and your father needed it I don't think we ought to grudge it to either of them."

"Mother—please—" Ralph said, heavily desperate.

"It's all right, Ralph, I've finished what I wanted to say, and in any case it's time the children went home, they mustn't stay up past their bedtime, must they, Sheena? I'm sorry this thing has been such a distress and embarrassment to you all." For a moment she teased them, sharpening would help before they went away. "I thought your generation took this sort of thing in its stride. What really upsets you is that I should take it in mine. And now I love you all very much and it was most kind and thoughtful of you to come today, and will you collect your children now and go away, because I would like to be alone."

When they had gone—soberly and it seemed to her reasonably content—she sat down, searching in her handbag for her handkerchief and found Philippa's birthday card still unposted. So she slipped on her coat and set off to the post office.

The air was cool, she had reached the gate before she noticed that it had begun to rain, but she decided to go on.

Drenched swags of lilac hung over the walls. Lionel and Boy were coming towards her along the pavement.

"We are on our way to visit you," Lionel announced, "and you are getting wet." He included her in the shelter of his umbrella. Boy skipped around them, playing a kind of private hopscotch. "I wondered if you would be alone."

"I haven't been alone. They all came. All the children."

"I'm glad. How are you, Julia?"

"Liberated. I never thought it would happen. Is Boy keeping better?"

"Quite well again. Where were you off to just now?"

"A little walk."

"Shall we come with you?"

"I should like that."

They walked in silence. Presently he asked: "What do you intend to do with your freedom?"

"I don't know. Now that I have it I don't think I may want to use it."

"You might marry me at some future date."

"You have a wife already."

"I feel sure something could be arranged," he said.

"No thank you, Lionel. We should spend the rest of our lives holding Memorial Services for Harold and Madge, you know we should."

"That wasn't really the idea," he said, but she noticed he looked relieved.

When they reached the post office she said: "Wait, I have a letter to post. A card for Philippa. It's her birthday tomorrow, it would be dreadful if I forgot."

"Ah," said Lionel, "so much for freedom."

She rummaged through her bag for a stamp and couldn't find one. Lionel supplied one from his pocket-book and she stuck it on and Boy was allowed to drop the envelope into the box.

"They have a lot of birthdays, Lionel," she said, feeling a need for apology.

He said: "It was fortunate I had a stamp. I'm not very good at stamps I'm afraid. Shall we walk back with you, Julia?"

They walked home through the rain without speaking. Dusk fell gently. Boy pulled at the wet sprays of lilac. Julia remembered with passion that Harold had been unfailingly good at stamps.